Tales from the Hill

Tales from the Hill

A Collection of Short Stories

Inspired by the history, geography and folklore of the Wrekin in Shropshire

Noel D Conway

Garmston Publishing, UK.

ISBN 9781791922153

Dedication

Thank you to Carol for all her help and patience with the manuscript and for invaluable feedback on the initial drafts. My thanks also go to Crispin who provided encouragement and some excellent ideas for presentation.

Table of Contents

Photograph of the Wrekin

Introduction

This collection of short stories was prompted when I was asked for a contribution to the local magazine *Under the Wrekin*. I had written a broadly longer version of *Cob's Den* for the previous Christmas season as a light-hearted ghost/folk story for the family. As it was referring to local landmarks, I thought it might be suitable and it was this that gave me the idea for the series. I was further convinced of this as a potentially good project when I discovered that there is very little that has been written on this area beyond the folk myths of *The Wrekin Giant* and that mainly for children. I was surprised at this because Shropshire has provided inspiration for some remarkable artists such as A E Housman, Edward Elgar and even JRR Tolkien whose depiction of *The Shire* in the world-famous *Lord of the Rings* is said to be based on this beautiful county. Shropshire has also been home at sometime or other to two major poets, Philip Larkin and Wilfred Owen. In addition, the remarkably successful *Cadfael* series of mediaeval whodunnit's by Ellis Peters and her impressive historical novels, as Edith Pargeter, set in the Welsh Marches bringing the character of Prince Llewelyn alive, completes a world-famous line-up of authors. Arguably, the most powerful exponent of the Shropshire landscape is Mary Webb, whose writings brought to life an otherwise unknown part of rural life in and around the Stiper Stones.

I do not pretend this work can compete with the aforementioned, but I felt that it set an interesting challenge to see if it were possible by using local landmarks and folk myths to contribute something to the rich culture already provided by others. Furthermore, I wanted to celebrate and share with readers the sheer beauty of the local landscape emanating from around the Wrekin and beyond. I am extremely fortunate to live virtually in the shadow of this impressive Hill, which seems to have the power to capture the hearts of so many locals and visitors. I have climbed it many times and sat and pondered the mysteries of life in the shallow bowl-like seats to be found in the volcanic rock above the Needle's Eye. This project, however, has produced an even deeper appreciation of the local geography and history for me that has been profoundly enriching. I hope readers will enjoy the stories as much as I have enjoyed writing them. I should say, also, that beyond reference to specific locations and historical matters of fact, these are works of complete fiction.

Noel D Conway December, 2018

xii

Wrekin 47 A.D.

Drogo forces his horse forward, flecks of foam from the beast's flared mouth catching in his cropped beard and Roman style hairline. He can feel the pounding of the animal's heart as he pushes it to the limit. Will he get there in time? Will he be put to death immediately when they see him? He has much to say but perhaps little time to do it in. If his horse stumbles now or one of these low lying birch branches knocks him flying in the dull light of a dying moon, all will be lost. The survival of the Cornovii depends on this desperate race to get there ahead of the enemy.

1

When he last left the Hill, it was 12 moons past and he was a different man. Gone now was the surly, swaggering irresponsibility of the younger son of a tribal chief. He had learned much of the wider world and of himself during his time in the south. His muscles had become hard from combat and his eyes saw more than they used to. It was the only way to stay alive. He no longer spent his days in drink or the company of women who were free with their favours, especially with the handsome young princeling. The Catavalauni welcomed the young, well armed warrior from the North who seemed undaunted by their frequent clashes with the Romans. However, it seemed to Drogo that the enemy were growing more numerous and increasingly difficult to contain in their fortified encampments. He noticed that whenever there was a full head on battle with them, they were never defeated. Their discipline and tactics were far superior to any of the Britons. He observed the amazing destructive power of some of their machines and marvelled at the swiftness with which they built defences. In areas of commanding, strategic importance he saw that they built in stone and brick. Some of these places, like Camulodunum, had erected high towers and were extensive enough to accommodate thousands of civilians. These were the Romano-Celts who adapted to Roman occupation finding it both attractive and rewarding. Eventually, Drogo's curiosity got the better of him so donning civilian clothes and tying his hair back, he went amongst these people to observe their ways. He noticed most of them wore short Roman tunics made of linen and the more wealthy amongst them wore clothes of bright colour, displaying jewellery of gold and silver. There was a great deal of hustle and bustle in the town with the buying and selling of grain, oil and many other products which he had never seen before. There were establishments for everything - brothels, drinking, buying slaves, clothes, ornaments of gold, pottery and silver, overnight accommodation and places to eat. He was astonished by the range of delicious and enticing food that could be had. He saw chickens and rabbits in cages waiting to be turned into the most mouthwatering dishes. He had never seen such before. It was a whole new world that the young Briton was slowly being seduced by.

What should he do? He felt like his old life was simple, crude and basically uninteresting. He obtained employment for a while as an ostler, sleeping overnight in the stables. As his command of Latin improved he learned there was also a written language, an idea that was completely foreign to him. He saw people walking around with parchment in their hands on which were markings that appeared to be extremely important. He discovered messages were able to be passed over long distances between soldiers or traders by the use of slate or parchment allowing the sender to communicate in detail what their wishes were with someone miles away. He began to learn the rudiments of this language. Drogo became increasingly romanised able to understand and converse with the foreign legionaries who were everywhere. This was how he learned that the Romans were here to stay, their prime purpose being to plunder the island of its people and resources sending them back to Rome, the actual location of which he only had a vague notion. He heard that those tribes who opposed their advance, were often wiped out, whilst those, like the Icenii, who allied themselves with Rome, became increasingly wealthy. He had to get this message back to his own people. When he overheard some soldiers talking about marching north and west, he knew he had to act fast, despite the dangers he may face at home.

'Halt! Who goes there? '
 Drogo expertly reins in his tired horse. He can't see anyone on the track before him but the command is unmistakable, confident and dangerous. The order is in Latin but with a Celtic accent. He must have run into one of the Celtic scouts from the Legion. He replies confidently,
'Drogo of the Dubonni. I'm returning home to see my sick father who is on his deathbed. '
 He knew this tribe had recently capitulated to Rome and were regarded as clients.
'Why, ' asks the suspicious Scout, 'are you lurking just ahead of the XIV Legion? '
Thinking quickly, the young Cornovii replies,

'I didn't know I was. If I had, I would have gladly attached myself to it in the interests of safety. These are wild lands and not yet tamed by the Pax Romana. '

This seemed to satisfy the Scout, who now showed himself by coming forward with his lance tilted directly at Drogo's chest. Nevertheless, Drogo's hand silently slides towards his sword. He doesn't want to be stopped and returned to the Legion. He grasps its wrought iron handle when, just as he is about to withdraw it and charge into the shadowy figure before him, another voice shatters the night air in an unmistakably arrogant Roman accent. He too comes forward but this time Drogo discovers he is outflanked and he feels the sharp point of a Roman stabbing sword in his back. It is just as well he's not been able to complete his move or he would be dead now.

'Dismount and lay your arms slowly on the ground. '

He has no option but to do as he is commanded. The Roman now orders the Scout to bind his hands and collect his weapons, after which he is ordered to remount and turnaround. The Roman peers closely at Drogo's sword noticing the sharp brilliance of its blade and the intricate design at the hilt.

'This doesn't look like the sword of a peaceful civilian to me, but rather the cut of a warrior. You will have some explaining to do when we get back to the main body and I'll make sure you do, 'he adds menacingly.

The three horsemen silently trot forward in single file, the captive in the middle with a long sharp lance at his back waiting to plunge into him with any false move. Before the threesome have travelled more than 10 metres, there is a slight rustling of leaves as two deadly poisonous darts find their targets in the exposed necks of the first and last riders. Neither of the victims utters a cry as they slump stone dead to the ground. It has all happened so quickly that Drogo is unable to comprehend what's happened until a hand grabs his bridle bringing his still trotting horse to a stop. Amazed, he sees before him a tall lean figure in the garb of a Druid.

'I am Arthfael, Drogo of the Cornovii, second son of Virico. And I know why you're here. ' The Druid slices through his bonds with a razor-sharp slither of bright steel that miraculously appears from his sleeves. 'You must get to your father this night and prevail upon him to come to terms with the Romans. Anything less, spells disaster. I will show you a secret way to avoid the other scouts but follow quickly and don't lose sight of me. ' Despite being horseless, Arthfael moved as swiftly as a shooting star and just as silently. It took all his horseman's skill for Drogo to keep up with him

Drogo arrives at the main gate of the capital fortress of the tribe just as dawn is breaking He has successfully avoided the sentries further down the hill by climbing the steep hidden paths he knows from his childhood, leaving his exhausted horse tethered behind bushes. When the sleep-dulled sentries see someone dressed as a Roman citizen, they sound the alarm. The doors are thrown back and a squad of well armed warriors rush forward to grab and drag him unresisting to his father, who has been alerted to the arrival of this unexpected visitor. When he recognises it is his son, he is both delighted and furious.

'Drogo!? ' Virico shouts, the anger rising in his chest as he swiftly recalls the details of his departure and his reappearance now in the strange clothes of the enemy. 'Why have you returned after fleeing in disgrace and why are you dressed as a Roman? Have you returned home to betray us all? ' Behind the fire in his eyes, there is also a deep pleasure that he is able to see his son again.

'My father, ' Drogo himself is almost overcome by emotion at this longed for reunion and his eyes moisten as he struggles to control himself, 'my Chief, I have raced as swift as the wind itself to be here to warn you of impending disaster. There is a Legion of the enemy not far behind who have the power to swot you like a horsefly, not even breaking step to do it. You must go out to meet them and ask to be placed under the protection of Rome as a client state. If you don't, or you show the slightest sign of resistance, they will crush you utterly. I know. I have fought against them and seen what they are capable of. '

Virico was still struggling with his emotions as well as trying to take in what his son was telling him, when suddenly there was a high-pitched shrieking scream and a woman charged forward with a dagger in her hand trying to plunge it into his son's chest.

'Murderer!' shouted the demented woman as she struggled to get past the guards who by now had responded to the attack. 'You should be flayed alive and stretched over an anthill until your eyeballs are consumed and you beg to die. '

It was his aunt, whose husband he had killed the previous year in a drunken brawl over a woman. There was nothing he could say but hang his head in shame.

'I know, ' he said quietly, 'but whatever you have to do to me, make your peace with the Romans first. '

Virico was impressed with his son's selfless words. He seemed quite changed from the spoiled young nobleman he'd been when he fled. Before he could respond, however, there was a further intervention from someone who could not be so easily dismissed.

'Look at him, the way he is dressed, the style of his hair. ' It was Caratacos, who was passing through to organise resistance against the Romans in the West. 'He looks like a Roman, sounds like a Roman and probably is a Roman. His words are treacherous and unworthy of a Briton. Don't trust anything he says, Virico, for he will betray you. He is a traitor who once fought by my side and then disappeared into the cesspit of the Roman city. '

It was difficult for Drogo to counter these words for essentially they were true.

'No! I am no traitor. Why would I have made this dangerous and difficult journey if I were? It makes no sense. '

By now, Virico had decided what he must do. 'There will be no alliance with the Romans. Our worlds are too different and their actions over the past five years show that they intend to stay for good subjugating all the tribes. We must fight to save ourselves from extinction. '

'But father, 'Drogo tried to interrupt, 'the Romans have so much to offer. We could become immeasurably wealthier with towns and buildings you cannot imagine providing us with a much easier life, where...... ' Virico impatiently waved his hand to stop this tirade of words.

'No! We are Celts with our own gods and beliefs. We know how these have been transformed in those tribes that have capitulated to Rome. We won't. We will retain our freedom and ability to think for ourselves. '

'Nor will we become slaves, who are the foundation on which Rome is built, ' added Caratacos clapping Virico on the back in agreement.

'Take my son away and keep him under guard. I'll decide what to do with him later. ' Drogo was led away to a small hut but he was sorely glad when his mother and sisters came to see him, bringing him food and solace.

At midday, Drogo was brought before his father again, who had decided what his judgement must be on his aberrant son. Just as he was about to pronounce his verdict, there was a shout from the lookout who began to ring the alarm. 'The Romans are here! To arms! To arms! '

Even before these words had been completed, javelins and arrows began raining down upon them in great numbers with deadly accurate killing efficiency. Roman scouts had disabled the sentries at the foot of the Hill and were now forming up in tortoise formation and training ballistae and scorpions on the main gate and palisade. Taking advantage of the confusion, Drogo escaped from his captors looking for his mother and sisters.

'Come with me quickly, ' he shouted, 'and bring as many others with you who are willing to come, especially the women and children. We have to get off this hill or we will all be slaughtered. His mother did not want to leave but she recognised their position was hopeless so she threw her authority into organising an escape. It would only be a short matter of time before the defences fell. They could see them crumbling now under the onslaught of the dreadful Roman machines. Drogo guessed correctly that the enemy would have encircled the summit fort and so led those who would go directly down steep hidden paths to the north. Once again in his hour of need, he noticed the Druid who somehow had thrown a smokescreen over the fleeing Celts. Meanwhile, Virico collected his warriors about him before one desperate, suicidal charge against the Romans. Despite their bloodcurdling yells, the Romans held fast, unbreakable behind their long rectangular shields, after which the short deadly swords completed the destruction of those that remained.

Silently, under the magic protection of Arthfael, the escapees of about 50 or so, reached the woods at the base of the hill where they were relatively safe, making their way to the great Sabrina River (Roman name). Here they collected in a copse resting, watching with doleful eyes the great plumes of black smoke which were now billowing up from the summit of the Wrekin. What were they to do now? Drogo knew there was only one thing to do but he didn't know whether it would be successful. Seeing a small troupe of Celtic auxiliaries, he stepped out into the open waving his arms to attract their attention and when they came closer he hailed them in Latin.

'Soldiers, I pray thee, take me to your Commander. I have matters of urgent importance for him. '

They were suspicious but clearly he seemed to be a Roman citizen and alone, so one of them extended a hand for him to climb up on his horse. They brought him to the camp a few miles away up stream that Aulas Plautius had established as his military base. He was surprised by the appearance of Drogo who then addressed him in perfectly fluent Latin. He could see from the tattoos on Drogo's face and arms that he was Celtic but one who must have been romanised at some point.

'Who are you? ' Demanded the Governor, for such he was, and more powerful than a mere legionary commander.

'I am Drogo, the only remaining son of the late Chief of the Cornovii, Virico, who has just perished in that battle. '

He pointed in the direction of the Wrekin which was still shrouded in the smoke of destruction.

The Governor looked at him sceptically,

'If that is true, why should I not also put you to death? '

11

'Because, General, that makes me the new Chief of the Cornovii and as you can see I have become romanised. The only future for my tribe is to become allies with Rome. I can offer you safe passage and guidance to the west in return for your protection. You may not know there are many other hill fortresses that I command now and they could be a nuisance to you, though I know, of course, you will be victorious in the end. I also have with me a small band of women and children survivors from the Hill battle whom I would wish to settle somewhere in the area. They are no threat to you and nor am I. '

Plautius was impressed by the young man's command of his language and his proposals, which he agreed. He would rather have client allies than intractable enemies.

The survivors from the Wrekin established a settlement next to the military base of the Romans. The settlement grew rapidly to become the fourth most important town in Roman Britain by the second century A.D. To the Romans, this was Wroxeter but to the Cornovii it was always known as the place of Virico, or Viriconium.

The End.

Historical note: In 47 A.D. the Iron Age Fortress of the Wrekin, capital of the Cornovii, was overrun and destroyed by the XIV Roman Legion

The Elf King

'I thank the Lord for his wonderful gifts to me and am glad to be given the chance to turn this hard-land into fruitful meadow, ' prayed Geoffrey as he toiled to lop down the sprawling ancient timbers that had been there since time immemorial. His father was an under-tenant for Earl Roger, and was responsible for the woodlands and a hundred field strips east of the Wrekin. He had offered Geoffrey the chance to clear some steep woodland on the bottom slopes of the Hill and obtained permission from the Lord for him to build a dwelling on it. It would be some time before Geoffrey and his new bride, Rachel, would be able to move out of his father's home in Little Wenlock into their own after he'd cleared the land. He was aware of how daunting a task this would be and the possible obstacles that could beset him but he was not to be deterred.

Geoffrey strained to remove the roots of the felled trees with the help of two of his father's serfs, Morgan and Rhys, who worked willingly with him as they had known him since childhood on the farm. Geoffrey treated them well and they shared whatever food and drink he had. He knew he had to really because there was little to stop them running off towards Wales and finding their freedom. But having been born this side of the River Severn, they felt half Welsh and half English and therefore unsure about their reception amongst the wild men to the West. In fact, they all shared a common hatred for their overlords, the Normans, who were now powerfully established throughout the land. Clearing the land was pleasant and enjoyable in late winter, ripping up the old, twisted pieces of wood which they threw on a bonfire, providing warmth and sensuous aromas of the natural undergrowth that sometimes intoxicated the senses. When the wood was cleared, the next phase was to remove the stones and boulders so that a plough could be used. Geoffrey knew how important it was to get the land ready for spring sowing or they would have no crop to harvest for winter and he and his Rachel would have to rely for another season on the goodwill and largesse of his father. He was far too determined to become independent to allow that and chafed to be able to start building his own house to begin the business of living his own life.

One morning, they came to the final obstacle in the field. It was a huge boulder, twice the height of the average man and just as broad. They tried all the known methods such as digging a hole around and under it stacking it with brushwood which they then lit. Then they took chisel, wedges and heavy mallets with which to start splitting the stone when it fractured from the heat. But it didn't because it was made of the same igneous rock as the Needle's Eye above. Next, they tried pulling it over using ropes and Shire horses onto log rollers so as to move it. Again, it wouldn't budge. Day after day for a whole week long they tried to move that rock but it was useless. Each night he returned home, Geoffrey scratched his head and pondered what to do. At the end of the week, he approached the stubborn rock once again expecting hopefully that a new idea would occur to him. This day, however, he found a figure sitting on top of it. A person the like of which he had never seen before. He was long and thin with a curious painted hat from which the plumes of pheasants, falcons and crows protruded. He wore a knee length coat of varying shades and colours on which seemed to be outlined strange designs that moved when he did. In fact, if Geoffrey had been more observant he would have seen that these were the outlines of people whose faces silently indicated pain and distress. Someone with the second sight would have recognised them as the tortured souls cruelly imprisoned by the mysterious creature before him.

'Good morrow to you, young sir, ' said the character in a strange and enchanting tone. 'Pray, how could I be of assistance to you this day? '

Geoffrey was at once taken aback by the chimera before him, thinking him to be an escaped serf or outlaw who, from time to time, would pass through the woods. He saw a long knife with an elaborate silver hilt dangling from a golden belt, so he knew he should not antagonise this figure.

'Well, if you really want to help me, ' he said cautiously, 'you could get rid of that rock on which you are sitting. It has plagued me these past five days and unless it goes, I shall have to leave it where it is, depriving me of a considerable proportion of my field. '

The other promptly stood up and jumped agilely to the ground just in front of Geoffrey. He was a foot shorter than the young farmer but his clothes and manner gave him a distinct air of authority. For a moment, Geoffrey wondered if he were a noble Norman, hardly having seen any, but then he remembered none of them spoke his language, only their own. This person was also strange in respects he couldn't quite identify so he decided he was nothing more than a vagrant, stealing the fine clothes and ornaments that he wore. Geoffrey was about to bid him good day when the other said,

'What will you give me, if I rid you of this stone? '

Geoffrey now thought the man was an imbecile and just wanted to get away from him without arousing his aggression so he said,

'Anything at all, my good man, but I doubt you can. '

'Anything? '

'Yes, of course, but I must now be off.' Just as Geoffrey was turning on his heels, the little man then asked,

'What about your firstborn?' his eyes glowing like red-hot coals in the dark. Now Geoffrey just wanted to get away from it at any cost, saying,

'Yes, yes... Now excuse me, goodbye!'

Geoffrey made for the two serfs who had just appeared at the edge of the field looking for security in numbers to get away from the madman. He tried to tell them about the apparition and what it had said but when he turned round, there was no one there but the rock. The other two thought he had been working too hard and put his comments down to fatigue. However, the following day when the three of them returned to the field they found the rock was gone.

The three then worked extremely hard until the field was ready for sowing in spring. When that had been completed, Geoffrey asked the hermit on the Hill to bless the field and afterwards he and the whole family attended a service at the little church of St Milberga's in Little Wenlock. The weather was clement that year and the crop grew rapidly so that by harvest time there was a bumper crop. Geoffrey and Rachel felt their lives were as full as they could be but they were to become even more enriched when it emerged that Rachel was pregnant. Giving birth was always a precarious time in people's lives then, but Rachel was young and healthy and she gave birth to a strong, young baby boy in late October. The barn was bursting with hay and the silos of grain full to

17

the brim. Geoffrey had been able to purchase two cows who were now expecting and a horse. His father was very proud of how he was making his way in the world and becoming a prosperous peasant. The manager of the Earl's estate had even suggested he might take on more strips of land given the success he had had with the first, especially if he were prepared to clear more of the thick wooded slopes surrounding Mount Gilbert, better known to the locals as the Wrekin. The end of the year and the beginning of the new therefore looked very promising for the young couple and they hunkered down comfortably whilst the winter storms did their worst without. That year was a harsh winter but Geoffrey was sympathetic to any of his neighbours who were not faring quite so well and generously shared his surplus.with the needy. Gilbert, the hermit, was often to be found in his kitchen warming himself by the fire with a jar of warmed ale to ward off the cold. Little did anyone know that these comings and goings were being jealously watched by someone who regarded himself as the Guardian of the Hill, as he had been for thousands of years. He resented the presence of the hermit and the foreign God that he served. His magic realm was not to be disturbed and he would see to that.

In the midst of one of the most vicious winter seasons for many years, the baby son of Geoffrey and Rachel suddenly took ill. At first, it was thought he merely had a chill and would soon recover but as night followed day it became clear that the child was worsening. His breathing became shallower and raspy. His forehead was burning up despite the cold compresses applied by his mother. There was a deathly pallor about his skin and both parents knew that unless they could do something quickly he would not last the night. Whilst his mother wrapped him in thick swaddling clothes, his father went to fetch his only horse. They had agreed the only course of action was to take their dying child to the Abbey at Buildwas which had an infirmary.

Geoffrey clutched the infant closely to him and urged his horse to ride as swiftly as it could. Before he had got half a mile he imagined he could hear the tinkling of tiny bells above the buffeting storm and roar of the wind.

'What is that behind me? ' he wondered striving to look over his shoulder into the pitch black night.

'This is absurd, there is nothing there, ' in vain he tried to reassure himself.

'But no! There it is again. Above the railing of the storm and the lashing of sleet, there is something else. ' He strained once again to focus his hearing on what it might be. Then, he heard it. A thin, preternatural, high, commanding voice,

'Stop! Give me what is mine. The firstborn promised to me. It is mine, mine...... '

Geoffrey couldn't make sense of the words at once but forced his horse to go even faster to get away from the demon that was behind him. The going was hard and very slippery in the snow and mud especially over the steep ridge from Leighton. The pursuer didn't seem to be hindered in any way and soon he was close behind so that Geoffrey could hear his devilish laughter and imagined the long, thin talons of his fingers trying to snatch the baby from him.

'You promised on the sacred ground of the Hill. ' The words were high pitched but unmistakable.

'A vow was made. A word was spoken. What was said cannot be unsaid. The child is mine… '

Geoffrey's body shivered convulsively but not from the cold, but the chilling words of the Elf King. He could feel some invisible force tugging at his precious burden, so he pressed his poor horse more harshly still to surmount the ridge and gallop ever faster down the slope on the other side.

'Come to me my child, ' the dark, seductive tones of the enchantment continued to draw the infant inch by inch out of his father's embrace, 'my mother awaits you at the soothing shores where we can play and sing in the surf. '

Now, the father had almost lost control and all seemed to move in a blur of motionless time. The Elf King summoned all his powers so that the rider was trapped in his time, his horse barely moving and the spell of his voice at its height. Geoffrey was on the point of utter despair when suddenly there was a bright flash in the sky followed by words shouted in a strong, full voice,

'In nomine Patri, Filii et Spiritu Sancti '

His strength returned and his horse was released to fly at its own speed onward to salvation. There was a great cry behind him and he knew something had happened to prevent the Demon King from carrying out his purpose. Now the journey continued as it should, but Geoffrey knew that his baby boy was still not delivered from the clutches of death. As he pushed his horse onward to the point where he knew the poor beast was on the point of fatal collapse, he saw the single light kept always illumined above the door for travellers at the Abbey. Incredulously, he had made it. With fanatical speed, he jumped off the horse and banged on the door until it was opened by the brother on duty, who ushered him in immediately as he saw the tiny innocent he carried. As he came through the door, Geoffrey glimpsed a figure silently watching from across the track. It was Gilbert, the hermit, and it was he, he realised, who had saved him and his firstborn from the evil of the Elf King.

The monks were well practised in the arts of healing at Buildwas Abbey and happily were able to restore the health of Geoffrey's son, Oliver, who grew up to be as strong and generous as his father. But Oliver was wiser than his father because he never, ever spoke words without first considering their implication, whatever the circumstances.

The End.

Historical note: During the Norman period, the Wrekin was known as Mount Gilbert and inhabited for some time by a hermit called Gilbert.

Death of a Monk

For Osmond, it was a strange but not unpleasant experience to be scrubbing pots and pans in the kitchens. It wasn't something his earlier life had prepared him for. There had always been servants at home and except when he was feeling a little hungry he would never enter such a lowly domain. He knew and accepted joyfully the commitment to manual labour which was a part of the Rule of St Benedict that the Cistercians followed. He was beginning to feel at home in the disciplined and quiet atmosphere of the Abbey though he didn't yet know all of the fifty monks and over a hundred lay brothers with whom he shared it. It was a magnificent building with large vaulted arches and beautifully designed tiled floors. It was the perfect environment to be at peace with the Lord, which he was beginning to appreciate more and more with the passing of each month. There hadn't really been much choice for him as the third son of a noble family but to choose the religious life.

He gradually realised that the other monks had finished their duties and he was all alone in the twilight. This was one of his favourite times after the evening meal and just before the office of Vespers at 6 p.m. As he luxuriated for a moment or two in the tranquility, he suddenly became aware of voices in a nearby corridor. This wasn't necessarily unusual because it was permissible for conversation to take place between brothers on certain specified topics, but on this occasion it was remarkable because of the heated intensity of the exchanges and, as the volume increased, again unusual, he could discern what was being said,

'What on earth are we going to do? ' exploded an increasingly irascible voice. 'It's absolutely intolerable and insulting to us all. '

The response came from a rather more unctuous voice, which appeared more restrained than the first although clearly sympathetic to the other,

'I know. This has gone on for far too long and we cannot, must not, allow it to continue. But you must keep your voice down and not draw attention to the way you feel. '

'This Abbot has no regard for the ordinary monk. He lives in splendid isolation, in a large well heated room and can go abroad whenever he likes dining and being entertained lavishly in the halls of noble families. While for us, there is nothing but fish, fish, fish - or no meat at all - for every meal. Our domains are overrun with deer and we have sheep aplenty so why does he deny us what we have always been used to? The reintroduction of the night-time offices, Matins and Lauds, is nothing less than inhumane torture when we are also expected to do heavy labouring work in the fields and quarries. '

'I agree, 'replied the less volatile of the two, 'so what do you suggest we do? ' There was a few moments' silence and then,

'We have no choice but to get rid of him and the only possible way that can be done is quickly and decisively. '

The two voices then drifted away out of hearing but the shocked Osmond was left in no uncertain doubt that the voices were planning something unthinkable in the monastic world - violence of the worst kind. Of course, he didn't know who they were or when or what was precisely intended. But he was stunned to the core at what he'd heard.

What should he do? He decided to observe the Rule which required absolute obedience from each monk, even at the cost of what he considered to be right or wrong. He would speak to the Dean of the Novitiates, Brother Harold. It would have to wait until after Vespers. In the even more darkened atmosphere and eeriness of candlelight, Osmond found Harold in the library. He was quite nervous about what he had to say but he found the confidence that came from being brought up as a nobleman's son and approached the Dean, indicating that he wished to speak to him. The Dean was no more or less kindly than any other but being in charge of the Novitiates, it was not unusual for them to approach him individually.

'Yes, Brother Osmond, what is it? '

'I wonder… ' began Osmond hesitatingly, 'could I speak to you in private? ' There were a handful of other monks in the library at the time and he certainly didn't want to share what he had to say with others now. Harold responded according to his duty, rising from his seat and ushering Osmond out to a small private office which he had the use of.

'Go on, my son. Don't be afraid. '

'Dean, I have something very distressful to impart to you that I wish deeply I didn't have to. '

Harold now looked at him with some consternation but said nothing, only leaning his head slightly more forward to catch all that the younger monk was saying. Osmond then reported as accurately as he could remember, everything he had heard spoken in the corridor. The Dean looked at him with growing astonishment and concern. He was aware of Osmond's noble background and therefore potential connections to people of power in the county. He could not dismiss him as easily as he might a peasant's son.

'This is extremely serious, Brother Osmond, and I commend you for having come to me. You have done the right thing. Are you sure, you don't know who the two people are whom you overheard?' 'No, I cannot think who they might be and I didn't see them. I've only been here a few months and there are so many brothers and lay brethren whom I don't yet recognise. '

'Oh don't be sorry, ' said the Dean, 'you have already fulfilled your duty. Now leave it with me. I will see the Abbot immediately as well as others who matter. It is just possible that someone may wish to talk to you further. I suggest you go and compose yourself in one of the Lady Chapels and then retire. '

As soon as Osmond departed, Harold moved as quickly as he could without running, which would have attracted unwanted attention, collecting together certain other monks amongst whom was the Dean of the Scriptorium, Brother Declan, and the Dean who commanded the laity, Brother Thomas. These were all senior monks. Harold immediately reproached his peer, Brother Declan,

'You have been indiscreet, Brother, ' he hissed. 'The young Novice, Osmond, overheard you talking in the corridor with someone, making plans against the Abbot. What he heard left him in no doubt about what's afoot. 'The others immediately looked worried and tried to say something, but it was Thomas who broke through the cacophony in a strong commanding voice,

'He will have to be silenced before he mentions it to anyone else who might take it to the Abbot. I will look for the first opportunity to do this without arousing suspicion. '

The others, including Brother Harold, meekly deferred to this pronouncement.

Osmond was in an increasing state of nervous anxiety. It was now two days since he had spoken to the Dean of Novitiates and no one, especially not Abbot Nicholas, had sent for him. What was he to make of this? He decided he would have to speak to the Dean again if he did not hear something by the following day. He put his concerns on one side temporarily as he immersed himself fully in the manual tasks of loading barges with woollen fleeces and packages intended for transport downstream to Bristol. He found manual labour a welcome distraction to his current worries and it was in this state that he found himself at the end of the day just prior to the evening meal alone down by the river filling the last barge. The late autumn light was already fading when he felt the most terrible blow to the side of his head plunging him into the midst of the dangerously swirling currents of the River Severn. He realised at once he'd been attacked from behind but there was nothing he could do about it. As his consciousness receded into a gathering darkness, he was violently reawakened by the intense coldness of the water. He found himself carried away swiftly into the middle of the stream where he began to thrash about to avoid being dragged under. Any older or weaker person would have been sucked under directly and carried far away downstream emerging only as a drowned corpse some days or weeks later entangled in the reeds that crowded the banks. But Osmond was no stranger to this river, having swum in it many times during his youth. He knew he should not waste strength by fighting against the stream, turning instead on his back he used his legs and powerful arms to reach the opposite bank some half a mile further on. Dragging himself up a grassy promontory, he lay for a long while reeling from the pain in his head. He began to feel nauseous, shivering violently from the cold. He had to decide what to do next. He must act quickly or he would die from exposure, so he thought it would be better to go to the Priory, which was on this side of the river at Little Buildwas, rather than return to the Monastery where he ran the risk of running into his unknown assailant. He'd no idea who to trust and who not to, so it would be a risk going to the Prior.

When he knocked at the door there was no answer so he banged even harder, realising that it was the hour for Vespers and the Prior and his assistant would be saying the office. A startled monk eventually opened the door and Osmond stumbled through in his desperately wet and bloody condition. The Prior, alerted to the commotion, came over himself to help the young monk and discover why he was in such a miserable state. They brought him before a fire, producing dry clothes and giving him something to eat and drink. It was only then that he asked Osmond to explain himself. As his story unravelled, it was clear the Prior was sincerely alarmed. He knew there was dissension amongst the brothers regarding the tightening up of the Rule by Abbot Nicholas but until now he wasn't aware that this was bordering on violent rebellion. He decided to go at once to see the Abbot as soon as Osmond was comfortable and his wound dressed. Neither of them noticed that the assistant had quietly slipped out and run as quickly as he could over the bridge to the main house. There he had immediately communicated to the conspirators what the young monk had said. Brother Declan at once ordered a message be sent to the Prior to divert him from coming to the Abbot. He was to be told to go to the farm at Leighton where the farmer's wife was dangerously ill and needed the last sacrament. Meanwhile, having conferred with his fellow conspirators, three trusted lay brothers were to be sent to the Priory to dispose of the meddling novice.

Another knock at the door of the Priory ensured the Prior was sent on his fool's errand. As Osmond dozed recuperating before the small fireplace in the Prior's quarters, there was more banging at the door until he had to rouse himself to answer it, there being no sign of the assistant. When he opened it, he was confronted by three rough-looking lay brothers with cudgels. It was obvious they meant no good and his spine tingled as a wave of fear flooded through him. Before Osmond could close and secure the heavy, metal-studded door, one of them wedged his foot firmly in the doorway, whilst the other two rammed it with their shoulders forcing an entry. The adrenaline coursed through his body as he recoiled from them adopting a surprisingly unbrotherly and menacing posture. Like a cornered animal, his eyes darted from side to side looking for whatever weapon he could to defend himself. His eyes caught sight of a stout lengthy staff, used to keep rabid dogs at bay. His heart leapt because he was well versed in its use as part of his military training as a young nobleman. Holding the staff firmly at one end with two hands, he swung it with all his might at the largest of the three attackers who took the blow full force on the temple and immediately dropped dead. The other two nevertheless continued to press their murderous intent but Osmond, elated with this initial success, now deployed the staff by holding it with two hands in the middle, thus enabling him to inflict fearsome blows on each one of his assailants continuously until they crumpled, unconscious at his feet. Before they could recover, he bound them securely.

He was now more bewildered than ever thinking the Prior must have betrayed him too. He was on the point of seeking out the Abbot himself by going over to the main house, when he heard the sound of a galloping horse. It must be the Prior, he thought. Returning back inside the Priory and taking hold of the staff, he prepared to defend himself again. As the Prior entered through the main door, Osmond raised his staff to bring it down smartly on his head, but on seeing this the other raised his hands in supplication shouting,
'Stop! I'm not your enemy, Brother. The errand I was sent on was to get me out of the way and I see by the three on the floor they didn't waste time in trying to get rid of you a

second time. There is something dangerously afoot and I think we need to act quickly. If you are prepared to trust me, follow me at once to the Abbot and we'll try to get to the bottom of this evil business. '

Osmond was wary but felt the Prior to be sincere, so he took the staff and the two of them took off towards the main house as quickly as they could.

The Prior was admitted immediately by the doorman, even though it was now after the office of Compline i.e. 9 p.m, when the community was supposed to have retired to their cells for the night until the office of Matins at midnight. The two scurried towards the Abbot's quarters but before they arrived a great cry went up of 'Murder! Murder! 'And the alarm bell was rung so that monks and lay brothers came running from all directions to see what was up. The person sounding the alarm was none other than Thomas of Tong. The Prior realised at once that the conspirators had already struck and when they entered Abbot Nicholas's room they found him stretched out in a pool of blood with an evil dagger sticking from his chest.

The Prior was admired widely as a man of devout and sincere piety who commanded respect. He was also known to be an ardent supporter of the Abbot's reforms as well as his friend. He was therefore carefully listened to by all the monks who were gathered now in the Chapter House where he carefully pieced together the story of the conspiracy, of the attack on Osmond and the attempt to get him out of the way. All eyes looked suspiciously on Thomas of Tong, even those who had been quietly conspiring with him.

'I'm innocent ' he pleaded, but in vain when one of the lay brothers claimed to have seen him being given the murderous dagger that had killed the Abbot by a stranger a few days ago. Thomas fled from the meeting and wasn't seen again in those parts for many years.

As for Osmond, he was widely praised for his bravery, but he sought approval from the Prior, who became temporary Abbot, to be allowed to go on pilgrimage to the founding mother house, Citeaux, in France. In truth, Osmond was not sure after all the events that had occurred whether he was really prepared to dedicate himself to the monastic life. It seemed to him no different from the world outside and he had been sorely disillusioned by his experiences. The divisions in the Monastery still prevailed and it would take a strong hand to bring the factions together. Whether the Prior was the person to do this he didn't know. He had come to respect the older man, but whether he returned was another matter.

The End.

Historical Note: in 1348 Abbot Nicholas of Buildwas Abbey was murdered by the monk, Thomas of Tong.

The Charcoal Burners

Luke followed his father silently through the wood. Not a twig stirred. They were past masters as woodsmen, none better. When they reached the water's edge, they slipped without a ripple into the freezing cold waters of the River Severn. They could see the barge a few yards away but only as a darker shade of black in the moonless night. Was there a guard? Would they have to fight for their lives in the next few moments and possibly even take life in order to do what they must? Luke shivered, and not only from the bitter coldness of the river, but from the thought of putting his mortal soul in danger. His father, he knew, had a long, razor-sharp billhook in his belt, whilst he carried his familiar hatchet in his. As a slight grey hue heralded the first light of dawn, he became aware of an accompanying river mist that rose as if to cloak their actions. Like a snake sliding from the swamp, Peter hauled himself slowly over the prow followed by Luke. There appeared to be no one present except for a bundle of grey and brown rags heaped in one corner of the barge. On further inspection, they could hear a low deep moaning from within and realised with a start it was the girl they'd been looking for. She was beautiful with long black tresses of plaited hair but they could see she was also in a desperate and pitiful state. Her dress was torn almost in two from top to bottom and even in the dim light they could see dark bluish bruises on her face, arms and legs. She cowered when she became aware of their approach but Peter hushed gently for her to keep silent telling her they were here to rescue her. He picked her up in his thick, strong woodsman's arms as if she were nothing more than a bundle of coppice branches and he and Luke then climbed out of the barge onto the rickety pier and thence to the shelter of the woods. If they met anyone now, they were dead.

How had it come to this? As they sought the greater security of the woods, Luke's head was awash with the images and sounds of the past two days. It had begun with the sudden arrival of the barge downstream from Shrewsbury where King Charles I and his men had arrived in full force a few days before, having raised his standard against Parliament.

Five fancifully adorned soldiers with the characteristic Royalist red sashes had been sent downriver to the foundry at Leighton. They were charged with loading the barge full of shot and other munitions for the Royalist garrisons further down the Severn at Bridgnorth and Worcester. Their leader was even more flamboyantly dressed than his companions. He was Sir Roger Liddle and arrogantly presented his demands to the lead foundry man. When he was told he would have to wait for at least another day, he was furious and cuffing the work man with one of his heavily ornate leather gauntlets, informed him he was on the King's business and unless he was obeyed immediately he would face summary execution as a traitor. Quite a crowd was beginning to gather around the disputants, drifting over from the small market stalls and tents, which plied their trade on most days of the week. The unhappy foundry man, Adam, stood his ground,

'No sir, we ain't traitors hereabouts. We are loyal to the King. It's just that we have just finished a large order and await the restocking of our fuel pile from the charcoal burners, which will take the rest of the day. We can complete your order early in the morning and it will be ready in the afternoon. '

'Where are these charcoal burners? ' demanded the officer..

'They are up yonder in the woods about their trade and I know some of them should be arriving with new stocks later in the day. '

Sir Roger was just about to order his men into the woods when the next sentence from the foundry man stopped him in his tracks,

'in the meantime, Sir, you can be well supplied with food, drink and even entertainment at our little market here. '

The Commander saw this pleased his men immediately and would put them in good humour for the rest of the day. Honour was restored.

'Very well then ' replied the officer, 'but at first light I expect to hear the sound of you working. '

During the course of the day, the five Royalists wandered around the market, taking what they wanted without payment, finally settling down in the drinking tent where they became louder and louder. Shortly after midday, there was some slight consternation on the arrival of Isaac Rosenstein, a travelling Jew, who was the first that had been seen in the area for many years. Accompanying him was his daughter, Rebecca, and it was she, rather than Isaac, that roused the greater interest for she was extremely beautiful and at 16 years of age in the first flush of womanhood. But whilst the locals had their curiosity aroused, the soldiers of the King had more pressing needs. They weren't content to look and leer but insisted on detaining the two, asking what they were doing abroad.

'Don't you know that Jews are not allowed to wander beyond certain communities without licence? ' shouted Sir Roger.

This wasn't the first time that Isaac had to show his credentials and he was ready for it.

'Yes, Sir, indeed I do, ' and so saying he produced a small rolled parchment which he passed to the officer.

'This is signed by Sir John Middleton, an infamous Parliamentarian and in arms against the King! This is worthless here, ' shouted Sir Roger angrily. 'Seize him and bind him until we decide what to do with him. '

Two of the Cavaliers grabbed hold of Isaac and began to search his bag and clothes, whilst the other two turned their attentions to Rebecca. At that moment, there was a loud commanding shout from behind them,

'Hold there! ' All of the Cavaliers turned round in surprise wondering who had the audacity to interfere. What they saw were two barrel chested men just above average height. One, a man of about 40 years of age with a long black beard and hair down to his shoulders, and another, a carbon copy of the other except younger and clean-shaven. They were dressed in woodsman's clothes of coarse dark green cloth. Over their shoulders were slung long heavy axes and behind them trailed a mule and a horse laden with baskets and sacks of charcoal. Sir Roger exerted his full authority by standing upright and clamping one hand on his sword hilt and the other on his pistol,

'What do you mean by this… ' But before he could finish, the older of the two woodsmen advanced towards him quite casually,

'These people are harmless travellers. What harm have they done to you and why do you treat them so roughly?, ' said Peter looking straight down into the eyes of Sir Roger Liddle.

'They are Jews, killers of Christ and eaters of children... The Pope orders no quarter for these enemies of the Catholic faith... '

'We are no Papists here, sir, and you would do well to remember that. '

By this point, there was a fair crowd gathered around and at the head of them were half a dozen foundry men who had come out to see what the fuss was all about. More charcoal burners began to arrive with their packs and fearsomely long axes. Luke gripped the shaft of his axe more tightly and felt the adrenaline begin to rise in expectation. He wasn't totally inexperienced in conflict. Ever since he and his father had left Hereford they had to fight their way out of a few difficulties when other nonconformist groups recognised Peter as a well-known and controversial Seeker (a form of early Quaker) heavily critical of their views. Luke admired his father for the clarity of his mind and purity of his religion. They had grown very close since they had lost his mother and two siblings to disease last year. It was the main reason why his father wanted to move away from Hereford because their ghosts were still real to him.

Sir Roger Liddle could see that they were now outnumbered by the workmen, who were tough, strong and possessed tools which could easily become lethal weapons. He told his men to keep their hands away from their own weapons because it was not obvious who would come out the victor in a fight. After Peter's comments about papism, there were many murmurs of approval from the crowd. The Royalists were apparently unaware of how strong a feeling there was in the area against Roman Catholicism, although there was sometimes equal strife amongst the nonconformists. Peter's views were already known by some around Coalbrookdale where there was a Friends' meeting house, which he and Luke attended from time to time. As the tension slackened, Peter boldly walked between the Cavaliers and led the two Jews safely out of their midst where Luke then released their bonds. The crowd began to disperse whilst the charcoal burners unloaded their packs. Peter spoke directly to Isaac,

'My friend, I don't think at the moment you are safe around here and I suggest you continue your journey as soon as possible. For the moment, however, with my friends and associates you will be quite safe. '

Isaac bowed slightly towards him,

'I had not expected to find such common decency and humanity in this out of the way place. These are turbulent times of course and it is difficult to know what to expect around the next corner. I have business in Coalbrookdale but shall be quickly moving on thereafter. I and my daughter, Rebecca, are deeply grateful for your protection at the potential risk to your own safety. I must say that we have found it safer amongst the Parliamentarians than the

Royalists, especially those we encountered here. I will certainly heed your advice. '

As the two departed, Luke felt a surge of regret that he probably would never see Rebecca again. He couldn't ever remember having seen such a perfectly beautiful young woman before. It didn't matter to him that she was a Jewess. He had been brought up to believe that everyone should be treated equally and with dignity in the sight of the Lord irrespective of what religion they professed. The only exceptions to this were the Papists because of their intolerance of all others and the persecution they meted out.

For the rest of the day, Peter and Luke, along with the other charcoal burners, helped to stack the fuel and load the furnace. It was hot, tiring work but they kept at it until all was done after which the foundry men invited them to have supper with them. The ale freely circulated but Peter and Luke abstained preferring the cool, crystal clear stream water from the woods. They hadn't been long at their meal when they were interrupted by Isaac, whose clothes were torn, and looked as though he had been badly beaten,

'Peter… ' He could scarcely take breath, 'please help me. Not long after we left at midday, we were set upon by three of the Royalist soldiers who must've followed us. They've taken my Rebecca and I don't know where she is or what to do. I fear the worst. '

The man broke down sobbing inconsolably, but Peter put his arm around him and drew him into the circle of friends where they gave him some food and drink questioning him in more detail about their attackers. Adam, the head foundry man, said he would enquire amongst the stallholders regarding the whereabouts of the Cavaliers. He returned shortly with a look of great concern on his rugged foundry-beaten face,

'They are not in the drinking tent so I have sent two trusted neighbours to spy out the barge. '

A quarter of an hour later, one of the neighbours rushed up to Adam and whispered in his ear.

Adam then signalled to Peter to come outside where he told him that the soldiers had the girl in the barge where they were making great sport with her.

'What shall we do? ' asked Adam. 'We could attack them, although there are only a few of us here, the others having returned home. '

Peter thought for a few moments then said,

'We must rescue the girl at all costs but we must be careful she is not killed at the same time. I have an idea. Let's get some of the young maids still at the market to go down and invite the soldiers back for food and drink when we should ensure they get so drunk they become unconscious. I doubt they will bring the girl with them so that's when we can rescue her. '

Having rescued the girl, Peter and Luke met Isaac as arranged at the bottom of the woods with Rebecca. From there they climbed higher into the foothills of the Wrekin to where they had their shelter. They had alerted the other charcoal burners to be on the alert for sign of the soldiers and get a message to them if they were seen. Peter thought it best that Isaac and Rebecca stay with them whilst they continued with their work, which would mean going down to Leighton so as not to arouse any suspicion that they'd had anything to do with the girl's rescue. When they did take a fresh load down to Leighton the following day, they found the soldiers had caused uproar when they discovered the missing girl. They entered houses and searched through every room and other possible hiding places. When they saw Peter and Luke they were in a foul mood and this time were determined not to be bested by common workmen. They were armed to the teeth carrying muskets and pistols and threatened to be more than a match for untrained men. Sir Roger Liddle did not believe for an instant that Peter and Luke were completely innocent. Furthermore, he had a score to settle with them for having humiliated him. He had his men ready with loaded muskets as they approached the furnace.

'You two,' he commanded darkly, 'throw down your tools and come here. I'm arresting you in the name of the King as enemies and traitors. You will be dealt with summarily. '

Luke surreptitiously glanced at his father and knew that he was not about to surrender without a fight. As his father swung his long woodsman's axe at the officer, Luke took the hatchet from his belt and threw it at the closest musketeer striking him full in the chest making the musket go off as it

43

clattered to the ground. But there were just too many of them and one of them had already shot at Luke who collapsed to the floor grasping his shoulder. Sir Roger Liddle had parried the axe stroke with his sword and was about to thrust an evil-looking dagger into Peter's chest, when there was a series of volleys from behind them. When the powder smoke cleared, all four remaining Royalists were lying dead or dying on the earth. Peter rushed over to Luke to inspect his injury and saw that he was still alive, but only just. He turned round at a sharp command,

'What's been going on here? '

 The lead horseman of four Parliamentarians wearing orange sashes demanded. Adam emerged from the foundry to explain that they had arrived in the nick of time or these Royalist soldiers would have killed the two woodsmen because of their support for Parliament. He thought it best not to mention Isaac and Rebecca who were hidden in the hills. The new arrivals were an advance scouting party from a Parliamentary Regiment from Staffordshire who were in search of the King and any Royalist supporters.

'It looks like we've arrived just in time to prevent further outrages from these Papist scum,' said the dragoon. Adam agreed to help Peter carry Luke back up into the woods where he could be cared for. Isaac had some knowledge of medicine and was able to extract the musket ball, which was lodged in Luke's shoulder, after which Rebecca took good care of him over the next few weeks.

Luke made a slow recovery during that time and Isaac helped Peter with the work he must do in return for food and shelter. It became clear that the two young people were very fond of each other and whilst Isaac was not so sure about a possible union between the two, he kept his thoughts to himself. Meanwhile, Peter had resolved to leave the area as it was becoming too dangerous with too many soldiers from both sides likely to appear on the roads at any time. He thought the safest place for them would be to return to Hereford and they could do that on the barge, which was still tethered to the pier on the River Severn. Adam agreed to load up the barge with munitions, which would be conveyed to the Parliamentarians in Hereford ensuring them of a certain welcome and safety for all: Peter, his son and the two Jews. It would be a perilous journey downriver because they would have to avoid Royalist outposts at Bridgnorth and Worcester but they were all agreed it was the best plan. Luke, however, looked fondly back at Leighton and the woods, which had provided them with a living for a while and vowed that one day he would return.

The End.

Historical note: During the English Civil War, Shropshire was a major theatre of conflict in the first phase. In Leighton, at the current site of the Kynnersely Arms, there was a foundry which produced munitions for Royalist forces.

Fern Ticket

Young Tom Shaftesbury had on his Sunday best as he bid farewell to his mother, leaving behind the small cottage in Steeraway Lane for a few hours of peace and quiet away from his younger siblings. He walked purposefully through the woods behind his house, where he had played and worked all his life. There was a certain restlessness that had come upon him over the past six months and he had taken to strolling out towards the Wrekin 'to get some air ', he told his mother. But in truth, he was keen to loiter by the Forest Glen with his peers admiring the pretty girls of his own age who were there to take tea with their 'fellas ', families or girlfriends. Most of them he recognised as old school friends and they nodded and exchanged a few words of banter, out of their parents' hearing. At 17 years old, most of them were in service in

Wellington or had jobs on the local farms. Sunday afternoon, however, was when they had a few hours of freedom during which they could think of other things than work. Most of his mates were on speaking terms to one or other of the local lasses, but as yet Tom hadn't had any success because of the crushing shyness which marred his handsome character. He was an inch or so taller than his friends with broad shoulders and a cheery smile. But unlike them, his work in the lime kilns didn't bring him into contact with the fair sex. He worried, therefore, that he would never find anyone to marry, settle down and have children with. It wasn't for the want of finding them unattractive. Indeed, he had spotted one young girl of his own age whom he knew distantly from when they were at the elementary school together, five years ago. He knew she lived in Little Wenlock, up the hill, where she worked on her father's small farm as a dairy maid. Flaxen haired, ruddy cheeks and full figured, some would call her 'plump ' , but Tom's heart always seemed to run much faster whenever he caught sight of Mary Hereford. Disappointingly, she never cast her eyes towards him and Tom always returned home at the end of the day with an aching heart.

One Monday morning, Tom was directed by his boss to ' get himself over ' to the other side of the Wrekin, where the estate manager was organising a coppicing team in the plantation. Tom had done this before and found it to be a welcome relief from the arduous monotony of working in

47

the lime pit. It would be a long day and he would have to climb the Hill to get there, returning wearily at day's end. On a fine day, however, he could take in the magnificent views that stretched for 360° around. Some said it was possible to see as far as Cader Idris in the West and, if you had the eyes of a hawk, the far distant Ural mountains in Russia. Unless the weather was ferocious, Tom always preferred to take the steep scree slope directly up to the summit passing the igneous rock outcrop of the Needle's Eye. Coming around the track at the bottom of the slope, he came across a bent old man wearing a large felt hat and a long cape that stretched down to his heels. There was an enormous bundle of firewood at his feet and, as Tom caught sight of him, he was trying to lift this onto his shoulders with the clear intention of going up the scree.

'Hey, old-timer, let me give you a hand with that. '

Before the old man could reply, Tom had effortlessly hoisted the burden onto his own shoulders and set off up the steep slope. When they reached the summit, the old one turned to Tom,

'This is far enough, my young friend. I can take it from here but I would like to give you something in return for your help. '

As if it were from nowhere, the old man handed Tom a small glistening fern leaf. Tom looked at the leaf and the old man with some amusement, thinking he was somewhat touched in the head.

'This is no ordinary leaf, ' said the old man, looking at Tom with bright sparkling eyes and a preternaturally young face.

'It is a ticket that will unlock the secrets of your heart. Give it to whomever you wish to share the love I can see there. All I ask is that it is returned to this place when its task is done. '

The ancient figure then swept up the load of firewood, as if it were nothing, and, before Tom could reply, disappeared. Bewildered, Tom was left with the small leaf in his hand, which he now looked at more closely. So far as he could see, it was nothing more than an ordinary fern, but without thinking why he tucked it carefully into one of his larger pockets. Over the next few days and nights, he didn't mention the incident to anyone at all but in his mind went over everything he could remember of what had happened and been said. The more he thought about it, the more strongly he was convinced that the old man had given him something precious. He recalled the words that were spoken and slowly a plan took shape in his mind as he lay there, unable to sleep through the hot summer nights. When he met Mary again at the annual Harvest Home at St Laurence's Church in Little Wenlock, this time he knew he would be well prepared.

The little church was bedecked with the wheat symbol from ancient times and, according to custom, the whole village and surrounding congregation brought their bounty from the land to display at the back of the church. Later it would be distributed to those who were on outdoor relief in the parish. In the evening, a barn dance was arranged in the little community hall that all the young people from roundabout would attend in their finest clothes to dance with their sweethearts or to search for their future spouses. September 1913 was no different from any previous occasion, except that Tom was now more expectant than ever. He had spent a few hours that day preparing a gift for Mary. In his hand, he held a small posy of cornflowers, white Campion and marigolds with the mysterious green fern leaf. He arrived early so that when he spotted Mary arriving, he could walk up to her to hand over the precious bouquet. What he didn't expect, however, when she did arrive was that she was with a few of her girl friends and he felt too shy to brave the group. He therefore bided his time until he saw that for a few moments she was sat on her own. Immediately, his heart in his mouth, he quietly presented himself before her bidding her good day and handing the small array of colourful flowers to her. She was at once surprised by Tom, whom she did recognise from school, but until now hadn't paid much attention to him. She was struck by the graciousness of his approach and the extraordinary beauty of the posy, which he placed gently in her white-gloved hand. When the music struck up behind them, he found the courage from somewhere to ask her to dance and she couldn't resist accepting. From that moment on, there was no one else in the room for both of them. At the end of the night, they agreed to meet next Sunday afternoon at the

Forest Glen and Mary clutched the treasured posy as she floated home oblivious of her friends' chatter and oblique questions about Tom.

The week proved interminably long for both of them. Tom once again strode out with a new purpose through Lime Kiln Woods though his heart was full of foreboding.

'Perhaps she won't be there? If she is, will she be the same as when they parted? When she gets to know him, will she still want to see him? '

He felt as though this was the last chance in the world to meet and settle down with someone, though he had only just turned 18 years old. Finally, he emerged from the rough track into a throng of his peers milling around the popular café. It took a little while for his eyes to adjust to the light after the darkness of the woods, as the strong afternoon sun forced its way between the thin birches at the end of the clearing. Desperately, he scanned everyone around but he needn't have worried for there she was walking quickly towards him with her face bright and smiling.

'I didn't think... you'd come, ' he said stumblingly.

'Why ever not? ' She laughed.

'Well I... Shall we go for a walk a little way up the Hill and then perhaps some tea later? ' Inexplicably, he felt more confident than he thought he would ever be. The words came fluently and thereafter with Mary he never had a problem giving expression to his thoughts.

'Oh yes! ' and taking his hand, she led him in the direction of the main gates.

 They talked incessantly, finding it surprisingly easy to be in each other's company. They reminisced about school days, told each other about the work they did, their home lives and what they might look forward to in the future. There were many other couples also making their way steadily to the top of the Wrekin. There were a few family groups as well with children running and squealing about. A few stopped off at Halfway House for refreshments, whilst others were eager to press on to find the best picnic spots. Tom and Mary were blind to all this, setting their own steady pace until eventually, they came to Heaven's Gate surprised at how quickly they had arrived. Opposite the pine copse, they spotted where the grass was lush and edged with ferns, which they both agreed was a perfect spot to place the blanket that Mary had thoughtfully brought along with some bread and cheese for a little picnic. They lingered as long as they dared before they realised it was time to return home, but agreeing to do the same the following Sunday, should the weather be suitable. If not, they would spend time in the bustling tearooms of the Forest Glen. Before very long it was evident to all their friends they were 'stepping out together'.

It wasn't long before the two were making serious plans for their future. In early spring the following year, they both pledged their troth to each other and it was agreed Tom would ask for Mary's hand in marriage at the end of summer.

August 1914 was an ominous year, but for Mary and Tom it promised the start of a new life together. This was the month they had planned for Tom to ask officially for Mary's hand. On the last Sunday of the month, he was to call, according to tradition, on Mary's parents to declare his intentions and make final plans for the nuptial date. When there was a knock at the door that afternoon, Mary raced to open it and there stood her Tom, but for a moment she was taken aback as he was dressed resplendently in khaki. He looked so handsome in uniform that her parents were equally impressed. Removing his hat, his shyness was about to overtake him when he caught sight of the fern leaf that Mary always kept displayed on the dresser. This granted him the courage he needed. He told them he and his friends had decided to join up at the recruitment fair in Wellington a few weeks ago, but he had kept it secret until he obtained his uniform when he planned to surprise them with the news today. They all congratulated him heartily and Mary was secretly very proud of how dashing he looked. None of them for an instant doubted that the war would be over by Christmas, when Tom would return and they could be married. Mary's father said there was a small cottage available for them not far away with its own water supply and Mary said she would arrange for the bans to be read at St Lawrence's where they would marry just before

Christmas Day. Mary's younger sisters were equally delighted by the news and threw themselves into the business of making her wedding dress and their bridesmaids' matching costumes.

A month later, Tom completed his initial training and was shipped off to northern France to join the British Expeditionary Force. At first, he had time to write a few letters to his sweetheart back home who daily awaited news of him whilst going about her duties on the farm. She poured over each of these missives for hours, sharing parts of them with her friends and sisters. She was increasingly concerned about reports in the newspapers of heavy engagements between British soldiers and the enemy, hoping that her Tom was well away from the fighting. This was the first time she became seriously worried about events on the other side of the English Channel. Tom's letters made no reference to these things and he wrote happily about the strange habits of the French who eat garlic and drink wine but who are very pleased to welcome the British Tommies at their side. At the end of October, Tom's letters cease and Mary becomes frantic with worry wondering what might have happened. She is convinced, however, he is still alive and that there has merely been a delay in the post. By mid-November, still having heard nothing, she is becoming desperate and doesn't know where to turn. Then, in the last week of November, she receives an official looking letter, which is from Tom's commanding officer informing her that he has been killed fighting bravely for his King and country at the battle of Ypres. All Mary's hopes are destroyed in an instant. She is utterly devastated but soon learns there are thousands of others like her in the wake of this massive defeat for the British Army. She stoically continues with her daily work around the farm and in the dairy, but she vows never to marry anyone at all, nor to look at another man, for her heart is with Tom. She moves into the tiny cottage that was intended for them both, placing the fern leaf besides a photograph of Tom on the mantelpiece.

Over the years that pass, until another generation readies itself for war, Mary becomes one of the oldest dairymaids in the area. She nurtures her many nieces and nephews who begin to appear as her sisters marry and realises that her love for them might have been the love for her own children, had Tom returned from the war. Every September, she walks to the top of the Wrekin, searching for the same wildflowers that Tom had made the first posy from. She notices that the fern leaf itself remains as fresh and as bright green as it was when Tom presented it to her. She also sees that in the full moon light, it glows with silver veins.

Finally, almost 40 years to the day after Tom had appeared in that fateful uniform, Mary feels an inextricable need to seek out the very spot which was theirs on the summit of their Hill. She also takes the fern leaf and a fresh posy of flowers with her. It is late Sunday afternoon and most

people have withdrawn feeling the slight chill of an early autumn breeze descending. She is weary and the long heavy years of pining have taken their toll. As she approaches their special place, she sees a figure in a large felt hat and a long weathered coat reaching to the ground. The figure beckons her closer, holding out its hand to her saying,
'I believe you have something there of ours.'
As she hands over the posy, the figure before her dissolves into the form of her beloved Tom exactly as he was when she last saw him. He takes her hand in his and gently helps her to the soft ground embracing her in his arms.

Mary is found the following day having passed away during the night, her face a vision of perfect joy and peace. She is laid to rest in the little churchyard at St Lawrence's still clutching the fern leaf that none could prise from her fingers.

The End

Folklore: Many from the older generations around the Wrekin often refer to the practice of courting on the Hill by asking, with a twinkle in their eyes, whether someone has obtained their fern ticket.

Cob's Den

In the dark tangle of decaying pine and birch that stretches from Little Hill to the steep scree chute to the summit Hill, lurks a legion of the damned. Malicious red and green eyes peer furtively between the sprawling tumble of the dying year. No one ever comes here at this bleak time of year, for those that do are seldom heard of again. Between the Eve of All Hallows and New Year, the dark spirits that inhabit the Underworld and the Old Year are at their strongest and none except those with hearts as pure as the driven-snow, can resist being dragged down into the depths of endless oblivion, should they wander foolishly into their domain. Since time immemorial, locals have given this neck of the woods a wide berth in winter. A beautiful and sunny glade in summer and spring, it is sinister and off-limits at the end of the year. Most people today don't know its name, apart from one or two old country folk, who remember with fear the name of Cob's Den.

In the tiny hamlet of Leighton, dusk was beginning to thicken and the dim lights from the Kynnersley Arms provided a welcome sight on this snowbound eve. One or two regulars had already arrived and were greeting each other cheerily in the light of the roaring fire in the great inglenook fireplace of the ancient tavern. Outside, emerging from the forest of the Wrekin, a tall, thin shadow materialised and crossing the road in long strides, stooped to enter the Inn. The stranger nodded to the landlord and took his place beside the warming fire. He removed his great, green cape and hood, which until then hid his features. His weathered, leather-brown face was no different to other countrymen at that time. However, the length of the silver grey hair that reached down to his broad shoulders, and the curved beak of a nose, suggested some long lineage back to the Romans. The clothes he wore were not the normal apparel, having an antique air about them. He had on a pair of black leather boots that came full length to the knee, as if for riding. His breeches were made of green corduroy, whilst his shirt of fustian brown looked more like a warrior's tunic than a labourer's smock.

The landlord brought him a tankard of ale, seemingly already aware of the stranger's needs. The latter nodded thanks and then took out a small, clay pipe, which he lit with an ember from the fire, and then sat ruminating, still as a stone, as though peering into a thick mist. One of the regulars at the bar, casting suspicious glances at the stranger, asked the landlord who he was.

'Who, the elder by the fire? Why that's Old Art. 'e comes in a few times at this time of year, but never at any other. 'e 's been coming 'ere since I can remember and I'm surprised you don't remember 'im yourself. I think 'e's a travelling forester plying his trade all over. 'e's 'armless and bothers no one,' replied the landlord, paying no more mind to the matter.

Beth and Peter, the landlord's children, had been sent home early from school at Buildwas as it had been snowing heavily all morning and the school was closed. The headmistress knew there was a danger of deep drifts forming and, as many of the children lived in isolated hillside farmsteads, it was important to get them home as quickly as possible. Beth was 8 years old and Peter was 18 months older but they played well together in the deepening snow until they became too cold and wet. When they noticed the dark shadows of the winter twilight beginning to creep towards them, they came inside going upstairs to the small living room that was the landlord's private quarters. After changing their wet clothes, stoking the little stove and adding two more logs, like good children everywhere they settled down to do their schoolwork. After they'd finished, it was dark, so they tripped downstairs to see their father busy preparing the bar for the evening trade. He didn't mind them coming down into the main lounge in the early evening whilst it was still quiet. He gave them some cold pork pie and pickle, which would suffice until their mother returned home later to cook the evening meal. She had gone to Little Wenlock to ensure that her ageing mother was well in this wintry weather and to take her a few provisions in case the roads became impassable. Little Wenlock was almost as high as the Wrekin itself and often got cut off in winter.

The children went and sat by the great fire to enjoy their tasty supper and found themselves near to the tall, mysterious stranger, who was still enjoying his pipe, gazing quietly into the middle distance. They had never seen him before and, whilst they munched happily away on their pie, they scrutinised him, unashamedly, as children will, and found him a person of great interest. Peter couldn't resist addressing him:

'Ye baint be from these parts, be ye Mister? '

The old one carefully retracted his vision from wherever it had been, and gazed benignly on the children. Taking the pipe from his mouth and placing it on the hearth beside him, he spoke to Peter in a quiet and friendly voice. It possessed an accent and tone which the children were unused to hearing; a dialect that was unknown to them:

'I'm from everywhere and nowhere, my fair ones. 'And, as he spoke, his eyes sparkled and his face filled with light. 'And I have known your father since he was your age. '

Both the children were bewitched by the charm of his voice and the love in his eyes.

'Then I bet ye know lots of stories', said Peter, hoping that the stranger might entertain them for a short while before they had to go upstairs to supper and bed.

'Aye, that I do my brave lad and some even from around these parts. Do ye know,per chance, that tonight is All Hallow's Eve, the most dangerous night of the year to be abroad? '

The children shivered slightly, but thrilled at the prospect of being half frightened to death.

'No, we dunna,' spluttered Beth, 'and why be it so bad to be about this night?'

'This is the night', said Old Art, 'when all the demons from beyond this world and all those whose hearts are as black as the peaty bog, from the evil they have done this year, are abroad. They go in search of any they might find, to drag them down into the eternal night of the dark chaos which would engulf us all, but for the light of innocents. Thus, it is not safe after dark hereabouts, to walk out alone, unless ye be sure your own heart is as pure as the driven-snow. For of these, the hoards of hell are sorely afraid. Around each one, invisible to the mortal eye, shimmers a light-green aura that will burn the evil ones to their very core until they no longer exist in this or any other world. 'Tis not until the Eve of the New Year, when the freshly spawned sprites from all the goodness in the world emerge to sweep darkness from the land and renew the earth, that 'twill be safe to venture forth at eventide.'

Though a country lad, Peter was no slow wit and he broke into the old one's tale to ask:

'Why be it 'specially dangerous round 'ere, Mister?'

'Because, my quick lad, of Cob's Den.'

'And where be that?' asked young Beth.

'Within a crow's mile of here, this side o' the Wrekin, and a more sinister spot in the whole world, ye cannot imagine.'

Unnoticed by his customers, the landlord had become increasingly agitated this last half hour and when the Queen Anne clock chimed seven, he exclaimed loudly:

'Oh my wife, Helen! Where is she? She should have returned more than an hour ago. I cannot think where she is.'

The regulars raised their faces towards him and one asked,

'W'ere she be gone, landlord? '

'To her old ma, up Little Wenlock, to take her some festive cheer. But she should 'ave been back by now and I'm sore afeared that she 'as met with some mishap 'long Spout Lane.'

 The landlord, beside himself with worry, ran to the door of the Inn and peered out into the gloom of the stormy night. The oil lamps that hung in the window cast only a dreary light for a few yards into the wickedly, blowing blizzard, which by now was thickly piling up the flakes of snow everywhere. He had not realised the severity of the storm outside, but immediately recognised the mortal threat it presented to Helen. Coming back inside, he took control of himself and the situation by calling for someone to take his place behind the bar whilst he went in search of his wife. This was well beyond his powers to deal with, but he knew he would have to try and even possibly die in the attempt to save his beloved. He called to his children to go upstairs and take themselves to bed whilst he was gone.

 Before anyone could move, a commanding voice rose above the hubbub of the room.
'Stay your ground landlord! I will seek thy wife this treacherous night for 'tis not safe for you, nor any other mortal adult here, to venture far from home with the hounds of hell in full fury outside. But I will take two here with me who have powers beyond their ken. I mean you two, Beth and Peter. Go quickly upstairs, put on your warmest coats and thickest boots for there is no time to lose. Quickly now!
'

As everyone stood around astonished at what was unfolding before their eyes, they saw Old Art take up his long, hooded cape and the old gnarled stick, which he thrust into his belt. When the two children returned, he grasped each by the hand and like a whirlwind left the pub with Beth and Peter at either side. It all happened so quickly that no one could intervene or object. The landlord was frozen and mute, still as stone. He feared he would never see his children again.

Beth and Peter felt no fear at all as the trio almost flew up the lanes to find their mother. The old man, who now didn't seem quite so old, knew exactly where he was going. He also knew that time was against them as they had well over a mile to travel uphill in heavy snow with a wind that raged against them, as if commanded by some dark force. As they passed through Neeve's Castle, they felt the wind relax and their spirits lighten. Old Art told them this was a fairy ring long ago and it still had some power at this time of year to resist the icy coldness that enveloped them. From there, they turned right into Spout Lane where the track ran level for a few yards before turning north again and dropping down. It was there that their worst fears were realised as they saw the family car.

 The small Austin A40 was stuck in a snowdrift by the side of the road and the driver's door was flung wide open. Snow had accumulated inside the little vehicle and there were no tracks in the road as the new snow had fallen thick and fast covering any traces of Helen's movements. But Old Art was not so easily deceived, and he knew exactly in which direction to go. He headed directly north over the broken-down stile that took him into the woods towards Little Hill. The two children, now gripped tightly once again in those great, gnarled, leathery hands, seemed to bounce up and down on each side of him as though they were puppets. The going was hard, but Old Art didn't waver, pressing on strongly through the deep snow and the tangled undergrowth. They reached the bottom of a steep incline that led up to a single stripped pine tree, where they turned right and shortly began to descend towards Cob's Den. Before they even arrived, they knew that evil was abroad in full force as they heard maniacal shrieking and cries for help, which they recognised as their mother's voice.

 The scene that beheld them as they dropped down between the trees was one that no mortal should see. Before them was their mother suspended 20 feet in the air being tugged this way and that by a hoard from hell: great imps, little imps, goblins and hobgoblins shrieking so shrilly as to rend apart the night sky for miles around. All were vying for the great treasure of the precious mortal, and the personal triumph that would attend them should they be the one to pull this foolish human down into the dark depths of endless night. The trio stopped for an instant only, whilst Old Art instructed the children what to do. He told them to raise their arms and run as fast as they could into the centre of the devilish crowd to rescue their mother. This seemed like madness, but then they noticed that each of them was aglow with a soft green light that surrounded their bodies and they remembered the words spoken in the pub, so they were not afraid. They ran bravely into the midst of the coven and heard the cries of devilish laughter turn from pleasure into terror as their hideous forms were shredded into nothingness by the children's power. As the evil army shrank back, their mother began to tumble earthwards. They rushed up to protect her and then took her back along the way they had come.

Meanwhile, Old Art took the gnarled club from his belt and the children saw that it was no longer an old stick but a flaming two-handed sword, which he used to slice through the bat-shaped banshees that were now rising with razor-sharp claws from the depths of the den.

'Run! Run as fast as you can,' he commanded. 'Get back to the car, where I will join you.'

The children did as he said, but they were in little danger now as the devils recognised how potent they were. Nonetheless, the fiends pawed and scratched at their mother seeking a hold on her to drag her back. When they reached the abandoned Austin, all pursuit was gone as Old Art had protected the rear sweeping away the last of the impish scum with his huge sword.

'Get inside quickly, ' he cried. 'I will push you to safety. '

As the children and their mother scraped away the snow and scurried as fast as they could into the tiny vehicle, Peter saw the flaming sword, still held high, dim and diminish until there were only little swirling flames along the centre of the broad, double-sided blade. He was sure, as sure as anything as he ever was in his life, that when the dying flames dissolved he saw the letters formed a word: EXCALIBUR. Then, they were off. Old Art had pushed them free from the snow and, with superhuman strength, up the slope to the safety and refuge of Neeve's Castle. From there Helen switched on the engine and, as carefully but as quickly as she could, drove down the lanes towards home.

I see from the look on your faces that you are sceptical of my tale. If you doubt me, go down to the Kynnersley Arms to check it out for yourself with the landlord. His name? Why, Peter, of course! But don't go out tonight, not until New Year's Eve.

The End.

Folklore: this is a completely fictitious tale making use of locally well-known landmarks and place names around the Wrekin.

Ghost Spitfire

Lieutenant Helen Worsley was nervous but she knew she couldn't show it. She had just arrived at the Wrekin Hilltop battery with seven other ATS (Auxiliary Territorial Services) raw recruits like herself, after eight weeks' training. She had been delighted with the offer of a temporary commission after she had completed two years of teacher training. The rest of the team were equally new to each other and their duties. At the tender age of 22 years she was now responsible for the lives of seven others as well as ensuring the efficient operation of a crucial part of the Shropshire East air defence zone. Her teacher training education had endowed her with a certain level of confidence and authority. However, she knew there was a great deal more riding on her appointment and their presence here than the others realised. Would she be able to measure up to these expectations? She had to.

These thoughts were passing through her mind as the army truck bumped its way over the rough tracks to the halfway station on the Wrekin, where she began to look around and appreciate the beauty of the landscape that was unknown to her. The other girls were trying to hold on to whatever they could without bouncing off their seats and landing in an undignified fashion painfully on the floor of the dirty truck. When they arrived, she was the first to jump out and take stock of the situation. She could see they still had a short walk to the summit where the Bofor's guns were covered by camouflage nets. It was a balmy early September afternoon with just a slight hint of autumn around the corner. A few of the deciduous trees had already started to turn orange and brown awaiting their turn to shower down on the ground below. It promised to be a lovely autumn, though Helen was aware that at this altitude it might be cruelly cold providing a further factor to undermine the girls' morale. They had already called in at their billets at Wroxeter to deposit their luggage but no one had thought to bring their great coats as the weather seemed so kind. They learnt very quickly that at an altitude of over 1300 feet, the gentlest breeze at ground level could metamorphose into a piercing wind above reducing them to shivering lumps of jelly unable to function properly. They grouped together and hugged each other for greater warmth whilst Helen went to inspect the installation. Everything appeared to be in order with the searchlight and radar equipment securely in place.

Just as she was wondering where the best places would be for her two spotters, there was an angry shout from behind her,

'Well, get to! Get to! ' An ugly, barrel chested Sergeant made his way towards her with a cigarette in one hand, looking as though he had just got off a horse. 'Where have you lot been? Stop off for some shopping in Shrewsbury, did you? ' He brought his full 5'8" up to where Helen was leaning over to inspect the equipment. She was temporarily taken aback by this loutish greeting but soon composed herself and slowly but with dignity stood up to reveal her full 5'10", so that she was looking down into the face of this red faced ruffian. He was immediately surprised at her height, which was tall for a woman but it was something that ran in the family and she had never found it a problem. She summoned up her most imperious look,

'Excuse me, Sergeant! It is a regulation requirement to salute an officer before you address one. Furthermore, it is forbidden for soldiers to smoke and a Sergeant should set a better example to his men. Put that cigarette out, Sergeant, before I put you on a charge! '

Sergeant Frank Bensley was not used to being spoken to like this, especially by a woman but it was the first direct command he'd received from a female officer ever. He hesitated not knowing how to react.

'Well, Sergeant? ' Helen's eyes bored into him like welding rods. She was not about to let this go. The Sergeant recognised he was dealing with someone here with a strong will. He realised that he could be stripped down for this and lose his Sergeant's pay as well as the respect of his men, which was lukewarm at best. For the moment, they couldn't hear exactly what was being said although they could read the body signals and knew that the Sergeant, their idiot of a Sergeant, was being dressed down by a young woman, albeit an officer.

'Yes, Ma'am. Sorry Ma'am, I couldn't see you properly, ' standing to attention and saluting her smartly whilst dropping the cigarette.

'Good, now show me the rest of the installation. I don't seem to be able to see where the latrines are, especially the female ones. ' The Sergeant was shamefaced,

'Very sorry, Ma'am. We only arrived this morning and were concerned to install the hardware of the battery first. '

'Very well, but I suggest you give that your top priority immediately. I would also like to see a demonstration of the guns in action, which I expect to do everyday. Furthermore, I want to inspect your men to make sure they are properly attired - in one hour. '

Helen gathered her ATS together ordering them to familiarise themselves fully with this equipment and not to fraternise with the men, who had other duties at present. She then took Charlotte and Sophia apart to confer with them about the best position for their spotting duties. As the girls go about their business, there is the odd wolf whistle from amongst the men but it is not obvious where it has originated. Deirdre and Beryl blush because they are not used to this having led quite sheltered middle-class lives. On the other hand, Betty and Maggie quietly giggle to themselves and surreptitiously eye up the men, a few of whom they find quite fanciable. However, Helen knows she will have to apply iron discipline or the battery will not run as a team. She has to nip this in the bud. She decides to strike immediately. She orders Charlotte, her Sergeant, to inform Sergeant Frank Bensley to have his men fall in whilst Sophia collects the ATS group together. Each group lines up adjacent to each other with the two Sergeants in front, facing her. She is a tall, slim and attractive brunette with a strong commanding voice, which she is used to projecting. She now uses it to full effect and cuts an authoritative figure. There is no hesitation about her and she extinguishes any self-doubts that she may have had.

'I am Lieutenant Helen Worsley and the Commanding Officer for this shift of the battery. I expect both men and women to respond immediately to the orders of their Sergeants who will be speaking directly for me. I have the power to make your lives difficult or impossible. You decide. Whilst we are on duty every person will be expected to devote all their time to the task allocated to them and, unless I have ordered a rest period, there will be no fraternising between the sexes, catcalls, exhibitions of strength or beauty, or any other behaviour which is deemed by me to undermine the effectiveness of this unit. I will deal very sternly with any individual, regardless of who they are, who ignores this rule. You should deem it an honour that you have been selected for this important duty and remember that many lives, including our own, are dependent upon each and everyone of us. It will not surprise me if before very long we will get sight of the enemy. You should consider every moment that you spend here to be equivalent to being on the front line. Anyone shirking that duty, I will deal with severely. I hope in time that we can come to know each other and be friendly but whether that is the case or not I expect everyone, man and woman, officer and other ranks, to respect each other. '

She then ordered a 20 minute tea break permitting people to smoke and to chat to each other. Hopefully, she thought, the ice is broken but she wouldn't know for sure until they had participated in action together.

There was a low steady droning in the background that none of them noticed until suddenly it became much louder and the three enemy planes appeared on the eastern horizon over Wenlock Edge. There had been no radio warning of their approach and the two spotters hadn't seen anything, which was something Helen would have to investigate later. The heavy Heinkel bomber with its two Messerschmitt fighter escorts saw the dummy airfield at Harley and attacked it directly, thinking as they were supposed to, this was an enemy airfield and legitimate target. They must have been surprised by the amount of damage they had inflicted judging from the columns of flames and smoke that erupted into the mid-morning air. They weren't to know that that was the idea. When those on the Wrekin saw what was happening they had time to scramble into position and the three guns opened up in their direction. They were well within range and made an immediate hit on the bomber one of whose engines started to belch black smoke. They were probably unaware of who was targeting them because there were no other planes in the air, but shortly one of the fighters caught sight of the tracer rounds issuing from the top of the Wrekin. The camouflage hid the battery but they knew it was there now and they decided to make it their second target. The Heinkel began to turn back hoping to limp home with one engine, but the fighters like maddened wasps flew directly for the hill after gaining some height and diving strafed the whole of the top of the summit. Helen ordered the ATS into the slit trenches as quickly as possible but for the two radio operators, whom she ordered to contact command HQ and request air support. This was dangerous work because there was no protection from the continual strafing which the two fighters maintained, back-and-forth, knowing their heavy shells would be wreaking havoc below. Like the other girls, this was Helen's first action and her legs felt like jelly, whilst she struggled to keep a steady voice. One of the gunners was already bleeding profusely so Maggie and Beryl, who had first aid training, raced over to the gun emplacement to get him away to a place of safety where they could tend his wounds temporarily. The minutes seemed to pass like hours as the deadly cannon shells from above sought their victims. However, within what had actually been only 10 minutes, a figure of four Spitfires dived in high from the south-east chasing off the German fighters who were seen to explode over the empty fields of Ape Dale. They then returned to formation and flying over the Wrekin dipped their wings in salute at the defenders below.

Harry, the wounded Gunner, would need immediate hospital attention and there was a military ambulance on its way for him. As soon as Helen was sure the attack was over, she arranged for him to be taken down to the base of the Wrekin in one of their heavy trucks, with Beryl and Maggie to keep him safe and comfortable. When she ordered stand down, the whole battery cheered releasing the pent-up adrenaline that was still flowing through them. Sergeant Frank Bensley, to his credit, came over to congratulate the coolness with which the ATS girls had carried out their duties under fire, especially the radio operators without whose brave determination to stay at their posts could well have resulted in considerable damage and injury to the rest of the battery. He and the men were also impressed by the way Beryl and Maggie attended to Harry. He suggested that at the end of the shift, they should all have a drink to celebrate their first action. Helen thought this would be an excellent way of strengthening both teams but meanwhile she had to talk to Charlotte and Sophia and discover why they hadn't seen the approaching enemy. In reality, they had been more interested in the local birdlife and had failed to spot the attacking enemy. Since they joined the unit, they'd always been slightly aloof from the others because of their class and their way of speaking which immediately distanced them from the others. Charlotte had been appointed Sergeant on the basis of some prior military training at public school and now Helen had the difficult task of reminding her of her additional responsibilities to the unit.

 She quietly took them aside,
'Well, what do you have to say for yourselves? '
 The two girls looked at her with a rather shocked expression having no idea what she was referring to.
 'Don't tell me, ' she continued, 'you have no idea what you've done, or rather failed to do. Let me remind you your job is to spot the enemy, which you have singularly failed to do today and it could have ended in disaster for all of us. I will not tolerate this dereliction of duty, which will result in court martial if it re-occurs. '
 She put on her best school ma'am voice feeling irritated that she did not have their natural arrogance and cut glass accents. But she was determined not to let that bother her. Charlotte was about to interrupt her to make some kind of excuse, when Helen curtly cut her off,
'Don't, ' she emphasised heavily, 'dare to interrupt an officer when she is speaking to you. If you don't shape up very soon I shall have you transferred as you are worse than useless at

76

the moment to me. I suggest you take note of the way the other girls behaved which was both courageous and exemplary. '

She then turned around and went to speak to the gunners before she allowed the condescension on the faces of the two girls to get beneath her skin even more.

After the shift, the entire unit headed off towards the Mytton and Mermaid hotel at Atcham. When they arrived, they found the public bar to be crowded and in full swing, as it was most evenings they were told. It was full of men and a few women from the local airfield and the surrounding search light batteries. Frank pushed his way to the bar and insisted on buying a drink for the whole unit and as they stood being jostled glasses in hand, he suddenly raised his voice and banged on the bar to attract everyone's attention.

'Raise a glass to a group of brave and courageous young women from the Wrekin Battery who fought off the enemy this morning, ' he shouted with a huge paternalistic grin as he waved towards Helen and the group of ATS. Everyone in the place looked up with happy, gleaming smiles and raised their glasses in their direction, the closest slapping them on the back and some shouting 'hurrah! '

A few moments later, Helen felt a tap on her shoulder and turning round found she was looking into the face of a young, blonde, good looking flight officer who by now was looking quite dishevelled and a little unsteady on his feet.

'So, you are comrades in arms? ' he said rather incoherently. 'I hadn't realised we had such beautiful comrades amongst us. '

'What do you know about this morning? ' asked Helen, taken off balance by this handsome young man before her, but finding his drunkenness unattractive. It wasn't that she was a teetotaller but she did expect people to be able to hold their drink and thought less of them if they didn't. He detected the slight coolness in her attitude and tried to correct it by attempting to come to attention,

'Allow me to introduce myself, ' he said as well as he could, but the words somehow got mangled before they left his mouth. 'My name is David… and we saw off your unwelcome visitors this morning. '

Helen was becoming rather irritated by this foolish young man before her and turned away to engage in conversation with one of the other girls. As she did so, another young man, also a fighter pilot from his uniform, but rather more sober than David, caught her attention as he helped his friend outside for some fresh air. A few moments later he reappeared and introduced himself as Neil Swann who was also part of the Spitfire formation in the morning.

'Please forgive my friend his boorish manner and drunkenness, ' he pleaded softly. 'I'm afraid he gets into this condition rather a lot nowadays. Quite a lot of the lads do. It helps us survive from one operation to the next. '

Neil explained something of David's background.

He was one of the few who had been at Dunkirk and since the start of August had been flying virtually non-stop. He had been shot down twice but fortunately managed to return to base unscathed physically, but it had taken its toll on his nerves. They were often over the skies of London, which is where they had been returning from that morning when they saw the anti-aircraft battery under attack. Fortunately, they just had sufficient fuel and ammunition left to deal with it. Helen learned to her horror that half the flyers in the pub that night would not be alive in two weeks' time. Neil told her that they were so desperately short of pilots they were being sent young men with only nine hours' flying experience and none of combat. They usually didn't survive the first few days. People like David were rare. He himself, he said, was also lucky though he had only been flying for the past six months. Inwardly, Helen cringed and kicked herself for her ignorance and insensitivity. She had no idea what these men were going through. When David eventually stumbled back through into the bar she made her way over to him and thanked him sincerely for his rescue that morning. When she left with the others, she agreed that David and Neil might be able to join them for a drink at the Wroxeter Hotel later that week, near to where they were billeted. They were currently on day shifts and therefore could be in the bar by 8:30 p.m.

Over the following week, the battery was quiet. It gave them all a chance to settle into their routine but command warned them to be on their guard as the enemy had stepped up its determination to root out and destroy the RAF so that they could continue with their plan of invasion. This time they had some warning. Helen had finished inspecting the unit and the practice firing of the guns had taken place. Everything was as it should be and she was enjoying the calm serenity of a late summer day made all the more beautiful by the wonderful views available from their vantage point. She saw the sun glinting on the River Severn where it casually meandered through the S shaped bends of the little Upper Severn Valley plateau wondering whether it might be possible to swim in its waters. The others were alert but quietly chatting to one another not expecting that this would be any day different to the others of the past week. The phone went and Deirdre picked it up at once. Helen could see it was something important as Deirdre's face drained of colour and then quickly came over to her to report that a huge flight group of the enemy were coming their way and would soon be visible.

This time Charlotte and Sophia did their jobs properly and reported in excess of a hundred bombers with accompanying fighter escort would be over them within 10 minutes. They were flying at 20,000 feet but when they came in sight it was as though a huge lid was sliding over them as the sky was dense with their numbers. They had never seen so many aircraft in the sky together. It was a veritable aerial armada. They dared not think about it but threw themselves into action. They noticed the batteries throughout the Upper Severn were beginning to open up and they joined in. Charlotte and Sophia began to take notes of which aircraft were hit for the record later, whilst Betty and Maggie hauled up more ammunition boxes around the gunnery platforms. Whilst the batteries were not the direct objective of the enemy group they were nonetheless part of the overall air defences and considered targets, so a few fighters peeled off to inflict their lethal reign of terror by strafing them once they had located their position.

But they weren't on their own. Attacking squadrons of Spitfires and Hurricanes began to inflict considerable damage as they were in great numbers from the surrounding airfields who had sufficient warning to get their aircraft into the sky. There were at least 60 Spitfires from RAF Atcham with similar numbers from RAF Cosford and Shawbury. The Nazi attackers, however, were not in a mind to cut and run. Their purpose was to shoot and destroy as many of the enemy aircraft as they could and they possessed some excellent pilots. At one point in the battle, Helen was aware they were under direct attack as a raking line of cannon shells showered her with turf and resounded metallically as they hit the guns. This was quickly followed by another and another as she tried to bury her head as deep into the slit trench as she could. When that brief attack was over there was only one gun continuing its stuttering fire, the other two were ominously silent. She raced over to see what had happened and discovered three of the gunners were clearly dead whilst two more were wounded severely. Without hesitation, Helen directed Beryl, Charlotte and Sophia with herself to clear the bodies of the wounded from the guns and to see if they were in working order, which they were. Deirdre remained with the radio whilst Betty and Maggie did what they could to make the wounded comfortable and safe from further attacks. She and the other three ATS took the dead gunners' positions and resumed firing overhead. The battle raged on for a further two hours until the enemy group was so depleted it was useless for them to continue and it would be lucky if any of them reached home with the little fuel they had. Some didn't even try, but ditched at the first opportunity throwing their hands up into the sky and being happily led away by young farmers and Land Army girls who menaced them with sharpened pitchfork and spades. The enemy had been stopped and the battery had acquitted itself well, though they now had dead to mourn. There was no trip to the pub that night as they were all too exhausted and couldn't wait to flop onto their cots in their billets.

The following afternoon, Helen received a signal to report immediately to Command headquarters in Shrewsbury. She had no idea what this might be about unless it was to congratulate her and her unit on their actions the previous day. She couldn't have been more wrong. She was ushered into the Colonel's office whose face was almost as purple as a beetroot. He seemed to be struggling with his emotions, in particular to restrain his fury which he now let fly as she entered,

'What the hell do you think you've achieved second Lieutenant ? ' he finally managed to bellow as he regained control of his tongue. 'Do you have any idea, my girl, what you have done? '

Helen was dumbfounded and couldn't think what action of hers could have caused such a response from the CO. On the other hand, she was not a person to be intimidated by such bullying,

'I'm sorry, Sir, I think you'll have to explain exactly...... ' She was not allowed to finish,

'You mean you didn't give any order for your ATS to take over the guns, or are you telling me your unit is so undisciplined they acted at their own volition? '

So, that was it. One of the band, probably Frank, must have relayed what had happened to his command from where it was passed on. He probably did it for the best of reasons, she thought, having formed a more positive picture of him in the last few weeks.

'There was no option, Sir, unless the battery was to be left seriously understrength when there were two perfectly usable and undamaged guns available. ' She remained unshakeable and calm.

'But you know you are here on trial. This isn't London and there are many people who believe the ATS should be nowhere near batteries, let alone engaging the enemy directly. It's not right that women should be subject to such dangers nor asked to shoot at the enemy. '

She responded patiently and rationally.

'Sir, there are many women now whose lives are in direct danger from enemy action and who welcome the chance to share this danger with men. Every day nurses in frontline hospitals, radio operators and clerks on airfields, drivers and countless others who are sometimes killed because of where they are. We know this and we accept it. We have been trained to operate the guns and can do so as well as our male colleagues, as I think we demonstrated. The Prime Minister's daughter herself is a member of the ATS and demands the right to carry out all the tasks required, including shooting the enemy. If they were to invade our shores, many women would take up arms and fight alongside their men folk. That's all we ask. '

The Colonel regarded her quietly, having listened to her carefully. He was impressed by her valiant defence of her command. He knew what she said was probably right and in time public opinion would support them. In fact, he was now glancing at a copy of the Shropshire Star which had landed on his desk whose front-page was emblazoned with the headline: *Our Brave Girls who Fight Alongside our Men.* There was even a photograph of the Wrekin battery! It was clear that public opinion locally had already changed. She also saw the newspaper and inwardly sighed with relief at the realisation that this was in her favour. After a few more moments, the Colonel responded,

'You may well be right, Lieutenant, but at the moment my orders are that you do not take up firing positions and until that changes I would ask you to respect it, whatever happens. That's an order, Lieutenant. Any further breaches and I will have you court-martialled. Do you understand? '

Chastened but not undaunted, she answered, 'Yes Sir. Understood. ' Whether she would or not repeat what she had done she wasn't sure, but for now to retain the presence of the ATS in Shropshire she would have to agree to the Colonel's command.

There was no action the following day nor any sight of an enemy plane. The unit, therefore, decided to once again visit the Mytton and Mermaid and celebrate with their new-found friends and colleagues in the rest of the area. When she arrived, she was at once aware there were very few pilots from RAF Atcham present. She asked one of the technicians, whom she recognised from the same station, who told her that since the mass attack on the air fields the other day, these appeared to have ceased and replaced by a concerted attack on London and other major cities. Consequently, since yesterday all the fighter pilots were on continuous duties fighting over the skies of London which people were now calling the Battle of Britain. The Spitfires in particular were carrying the brunt of the effort and the pilots were often returning three or four times in a day after re-arming and refuelling. They were exhausted and the losses were extremely high. Just as she was about to leave, she saw Flight Lieutenant Neil Swan enter. He was haggard and drawn but tried to put on a cheerful face when he saw Helen.

'Where's David? ' she asked immediately and when his attempt at cheerfulness turned to a frown, she felt butterflies in her stomach. She hadn't realised what her feelings were for David, but now she was on the verge of panic - a completely new sensation for her.

'I'm afraid, ' said his friend, 'he hasn't yet returned ' adding immediately, 'but that doesn't mean to say he won't. He could well have been forced to bail out and will probably turn up tomorrow or the day after demanding a new Spitfire. '

'Neil, ' she said desperately, ' please let me know as soon as he does or… ' She didn't want to say the words but she didn't have to. Neil nodded and hugged her comfortingly.

Neil was right and David did materialise two days later after having bailed out without a scratch somewhere over north London from where he managed to hitch a ride home. Learning of Helen's enquiries, David borrows a motorbike and visits her while she is on duty at the battery. As soon as she sees him, she throws caution to the wind and launches herself into his arms. The rest of the unit cheer and quietly resume their duties whilst the two lovers recover themselves. David suddenly breaks away from the embrace, angry with himself at his loss of control,

'No, no. I can't do this, ' he wrestles with himself whilst Helen looks on hurt and bewildered. 'It's just not right, ' he says, almost weeping, 'I may be dead in a day or two. It's not right that I should allow you to feel this way for me… ' He can't go on.

Helen realises at once, what the problem is,

'David, my love, if that happens, it happens. We cannot deny what we feel towards each other, nor should we. This damned war should not come between us. Let us live in hope, always, as so many others are doing too. I love you and I want to be with you. I too could be dead any day but I'm not going to let that extinguish my feelings. '

'But you don't understand, ' he says with anguish, the tears rolling down his cheeks, 'I have exhausted my nine lives and it is only a matter of time now - a very short space of time. I should not be so selfish. '

She embraces him even more tightly, stroking his hair and looking deep into his eyes says,

'You cannot leave me - now or ever. You are too firmly lodged in my heart. Let it be. '

He looks at her like a stray kitten which has just returned safely home. He cannot resist her plea and buries his head in her bosom in a spasm of weeping. They stay like this for half an hour or more and then they become aware of where they are and that David must return. The battle calls.

Two days later, towards late afternoon, Helen is sadly reflecting on how all their lives are not their own. There have been no further encounters with the enemy and all has been quiet. Imperceptibly at first, she becomes aware of a slight droning in the distance and as it gets closer, the unmistakable constant soft stuttering of a Spitfire's Rolls-Royce Merlin engine becomes louder and louder. She looks up into the soft light blue haze and sees the unique outline as it comes towards her, where reaching the summit, dips its wings in salute and flies off into the West its sound diminishing. She recognises the markings of RAF Atcham and wonders for a moment why it is not going north-west. She thinks nothing more of it until the radio telephone rings an hour later and Beryl quietly says it's for her. It's the Adjutant at the base who has called with the inevitable news that David has been shot down and his Spitfire was seen to explode immediately with no chance of bailing out. She cannot move and Beryl gently takes the handset from her. Helen somehow finds the inner strength to carry on, one day after another, but for days and even months later she is haunted at the end of the day by the sound of the Merlin engine getting louder and louder and then diminishing. When she looks up, there is nothing there, but she is comforted with the thought that it is David.

The End.

Folklore: Obscure references can be found referring to the noise of a Spitfire engine over the Wrekin and the sighting of strange vapour trails. Some believe these are spectral signs of a fatal crash by an Australian Spitfire pilot in 1941 on Little Hill after his return from a sortie.

The Beacon

Bill wasn't asleep. He could never sleep now. His life was in ruins and he pined for his sweetheart whom he knew he would never see again. On the testimony of false witness, he had been accused of brutally raping her and must serve 10 years as punishment. Worst of all, however, was that he had been inside six months now, and written to her several times, without receiving a single reply. Could it be, that she really felt he was guilty of what he was accused? He washed and shaved only because it was automatic and he shovelled the savourless food into himself because there was nothing else to do. There was only one bright moment in his existence when Martin, his identical twin, came to visit. Martin shared Bill's loss as if it had been his own. The brothers had always had this unnerving bond between them. Most people couldn't tell the difference between them and Martin sometimes found it difficult getting out of the prison after visits as the warders believed it was merely an escape attempt by Bill. In the end, he had to take his ration card to prove who he was.

Lying on his cot, dozing in the half light of his tiny cell, he became aware of a blinking red shadow, which must have been there all along but that he hadn't noticed, preoccupied as he was with the friendless world without and his feelings of utter powerlessness within. Listless but curious, he shifted the single chair that represented his sole possession to beneath the small barred, rectangular window that provided a modicum of light during the day. If he stood on the chair, he could just about see out. There it was, the red shadow that was stirring something inside him trying to make him connect with reality. It was the silently pulsating beacon on the Wrekin, clearly visible from his high cell in Shrewsbury prison, a sentinel to warn planes of its erratic mass which, in the five years since it was erected, still acted as a merciless Cyrene drawing men to their deaths like moths to a lamp. He knew the beacon was meant to counteract this sinister trap and it had doubtless saved many lives as the skies of wartime Britain became dangerously overcrowded. What would its effect be on him? He gazed at it for a long time mesmerised by its mind emptying qualities. Then a thought like lightning energised his whole body. He knew what to do. He must escape and follow the light that would take him to Julia whose torment he could not imagine and didn't want to. Since Mrs Johnson, her

91

guardian, had died a year ago from cancer, she had been subjected to an increasingly hostile home. The farmer cared little about her and always had since she had been billeted on them as an evacuee from London in 1941. He resented her presence as an unpaying guest, especially when they learned her parents had been killed in the Blitz and Mrs Johnson wanted to keep her on as a substitute for the daughter she had always wanted. Over the years, Frank, the Johnson's only son, an oversized oaf of a boy, grew up to become a menacing and vicious presence. Whenever he could, he would bully her, accusing her of some misdemeanour of which she was innocent. Since his mother's death, however, and Julia's blossoming womanhood, he began to exhibit a lurid and unwanted interest in her. Bill's nightmares were populated by images of Frank leering lasciviously at his sweetheart.

Martin came to visit the following afternoon. Bill was a completely changed man, which Martin felt immediately he entered the room. Gone was the hopeless look of despair and even the gaunt features that had developed over the past few months, as Bill reluctantly kept himself alive, made him look sharper and more alert. As he sat down, Martin knew Bill had a plan and they both waited for the moment when they would not be overheard by the ever vigilant warders.
'Martin, ' hissed Bill, 'I have to get out of here. I have to see Julia and find out what's happening to her. '

All this was spoken between normal conversation. He asked Martin to obtain a small, strong file for him, smuggling it in hidden in a thick magazine in a way that it wouldn't be detected. He then outlined the rest of the plan and when he was ready, Martin agreed to be waiting for him on the outer walls of the prison.

It was going to take Bill some time to file through the iron bars of his little window and he would have to be extremely vigilant that he wasn't heard or seen. He plotted the times the warders peered through his spy hole, particularly at night, when he discovered they only did so three times and each time was the same - they valued their sleep too much. He was also careful to find a hiding place for the file, which he did in the tubular bed of the cot. He measured the cell window and knew that if he could get his shoulders through it would be big enough for the rest of him. He felt at once anxious and excited by his endeavours, but he realised he would only have the one chance because if he were caught trying to escape he would be sent to a much more secure prison. He was also aware that Julia could be in constant danger amongst the Johnsons though he didn't dwell on what form that might take. He forced himself to focus on his primary objective and the continual need for remaining alert, which sustained him through the worst moments of his anxieties.

Within a month he was ready, and told Martin to be waiting for him. He chose a night of the new moon when the weather report predicted heavy cloud and moderate rain. After the second check at 3 o'clock in the morning by the prison officers, he was ready with the torn strips from his sheets and blankets to attempt his daring escape. He left one iron bar securely in place around which he fastened a strip of cotton sheet. The next part was particularly difficult as he had to exit feet first with one hand on the sheet. He had thought about this carefully and knew it could only be achieved if he were facing down but how was he going to get in that position? The chair was too short so there was no option but to lean his iron cot vertically against the wall under the window and push himself up into the opening with his arms. This would take some considerable power so he'd been strengthening his deteriorating muscles - a consequence of having no regular physical labour inside - by a regime of press ups and pull-ups under his bed. He felt particularly exposed as he got his feet through the little window and then gradually more of his body up to his behind. He felt the top of the frame and the stumps of the bars digging deeply into his buttocks as he shimmied his way slowly out. He knew he couldn't take too long about this dangerous manoeuvre because in two hours there would be another check at the spy hole. Each minute it took meant one less minute to escape on the ground and the closer he was to the prison the greater the likelihood of recapture.

Slowly, hand over hand, his heart pumping 20 to the dozen, he felt his legs gripped.

Martin steadied the final part of his descent. They crossed the road quickly to a side street where the second phase of the plan was executed. The two brothers embraced silently and parted. Martin threaded his way stealthily through alleyways and small streets northwards. Bill turned east locating the fixed point of his destination. He knew where the river was close by and from there he followed a well hidden path out of the city in a north-easterly direction. He still had an hour left before he reckoned the alarm would go up, so like a phantom he passed unseen and unheard through the tiny villages of Uffington and Upton Magna as he raced as fast as he could towards the Wrekin. However, by the time he reached the A5 dawn was already casting long shadows, as the easterly sun rose. Alarmingly, early traffic was beginning to stream along this major east-west conduit. He still could not risk being seen and guessed by now the manhunt was in full swing, soon confirmed by two black police cars with sirens flashing speeding towards Wellington. Seeing a derelict barn close by the field, he decided to hide away there until nightfall.

Martin knew this part of Shrewsbury well as he often made deliveries to the local shops from the warehouse where he worked in the centre of town. Unlike Bill, Martin was a townie and travelled there daily by train from Wellington.

At some stage, he thought, he would like to find a flat there but for the moment, until he too was called up for National Service, he would grit his teeth and continue to live in the parental home. He realised he could lose his job by helping his brother in this way but felt that he had no choice. Bill had been unjustly condemned and needed every chance to clear himself. He was cold and shivering in the prison stripes and, though he avoided people for as long as possible, it was important to look like an escaped convict to take the hunt from his brother. He knew it wouldn't be long before he was apprehended, when daylight revealed the secrets of the night, but he hoped to give Bill a good chance, so when he reached Battlefield he took the small paths and kept close to the hedges. It was inevitable they would concentrate the search north of the city where a number of important roads led off in various directions and it was difficult for him to avoid being seen from this thick cluster of roads. He heard them well before he saw anything. Police sirens and whistles seemed to swirl all around him and he wasn't sure in which direction they would come for him. In truth, they were on three sides and were in hot pursuit towards him over the fields. Nevertheless, he doggedly maintained his flight, jumping over fences and struggling to force his way through brambles and clusters of stinging nettles. Eventually he was literally brought to bay by police dogs who cornered him in a field, nipping his heels if he moved and displaying fearsome slavering fangs as though they were the Baskerville hounds. He dared not move and it felt that at any moment he could be torn to shreds. A few moments later he was relieved when an officer handcuffed him and led him away.

He was returned immediately to the prison and brought before the Governor who interrogated him.

'Prisoner 471, you have led us a merry dance and your sentence will be extended as a result, ' he said sternly with a hint of anger. His tone then changed to a more compassionate one,

'Bill, why have you done this? You know I was sympathetic to reopening your case because I felt that something wasn't quite right. From the moment I saw you, I couldn't bring myself to believe that you are a rapist. And why you should rape your fiancé just doesn't make sense. Of course, the presence of your pocketknife at the scene and the witness statement of the farmer's son were damning. '

Since his capture, Martin had remained silent but now he felt moved to say something in mitigation of his brother's actions.

'I'm innocent, Governor, and will maintain that if I have to stay in this place until I rot in hell. '

Instantly, the Governor sensed there was something different about 'Bill '. There was something about the quality and strength of the voice, which seemed thinner and weaker than the one he was used to. He scrutinised the man before him more closely and noticed he was less gaunt than his erstwhile prisoner. He had Bill's file before him so he now opened it. Of course, how stupid, it was staring him right in the face. Bill Briers has an identical twin, but which one is before him?

'Very clever, ' the hardness in his tone returns. The Governor does not like to be hoodwinked and shown to be a fool.

'So Martin! ' He spits out the name sharply but Martin doesn't flinch. He has expected this and he will try to maintain the deception for as long as he can.

'It is a felony to aid and abet an escaping prisoner. You could go to prison for this. '

Martin calmly looks at the Governor with a slightly quizzical smile,

'You are mistaken, Governor, I am Bill. My brother will be hard at work now and he knows nothing about this. '

'We'll see about that, ' replies the Governor angrily. He picks up his telephone and curtly demands to be put through too Inspector Walsh at Shrewsbury police station. When the other answers, he quickly appraises him of the deception and requests that Mr and Mrs Briers be picked up at once from their Wellington home and brought immediately to the prison. He knows that the definitive identification can only be made by the parents. Martin betrays no qualms about this and is placed in Bill's cell awaiting their arrival. It is a novelty for him and he begins to feel what his brother must have gone through over the past six months confined to this tiny, shadowy, cold room. He shivers involuntarily and imagines that he may have to get used to something like this as a punishment. Within an hour he is sitting once again in the Governor's office where Mr and Mrs Briers have been told what they must do. They both have steaming mugs of tea in their hands and whilst they make small talk until the prisoner arrives, the Governor notices how unsympathetic they appear to be towards whichever of their sons is in front of him. They recognise Martin immediately and the ruse is confirmed. The Governor quickly orders the resumption of the search feeling angry and impatient with everyone around but particularly with himself. Martin continues to refuse to answer any further questions but the Governor instinctively feels that Bill maybe heading in the direction of the Johnson's farm under the Wrekin.

When dusk descends, Bill stealthily crosses the road into the small lanes that will take him to the place he knows so well. He can see lights glaring through the curtainless windows from the farm kitchen and makes his way carefully towards the barn adjacent to the main building. He sees Step, the farm dog, who recognises him at once from a distance and happily runs towards him without making a sound in expectation of the genuine fondling that she knows she will get from Bill. He decides to hideaway in the loft so he can observe what's going on both in the yard and the barn. It's lucky that Martin thought to provide him with a little food otherwise he would be absolutely famished by now, but his stomach still growls as he smells the delicious food that Julia will have made for the men. Not long afterwards, his heart aches as he sees her profile at the kitchen window clearing the scraps and washing up. He longs to rush out and take her in his arms but he daren't do this because he knows he will meet a violent reaction from the Johnsons.

An hour later, Julia emerges and comes into the barn to obtain some hay for the dairy cows. A few minutes later, he notices that Frank follows her out and into the barn where he approaches her from behind as she collects the hay together. He grabs her tightly from behind which sends the pitchfork flying and then throws her roughly onto her back on the heaped up hay. He steps forward to snatch her dress up from her knees and with a leering sneer throws himself on top of her as she fights to keep him off. As he scrabbles with his belt and holds her down, two outraged hands grab him from behind and haul him off the hysterical girl with superhuman strength. Bill's face is pulsating with anger and he feels all the pent-up injustice since the accusation and trial flow through his body like an erupting volcano. He pounds into Frank mercilessly pummelling him with his fists making a bloody mess of his face so that even if the bully wanted to resist he physically couldn't. At that moment, a shot shatters the night air and both young men look around startled to see Mr Johnson with his shotgun which he is now pointing at Bill.

'Get off my son, you animal! What do you think you're doing? '

'It's not me who is the animal here, and you are no better turning a blind eye to what must have been obvious to anyone. She should never have been left here alone with the likes of you two. '

'Get up and move over there, where I can get a better shot of you without hitting my son. The police will thank me for having stopped a dangerous prisoner on the loose. '

The farmer raises his shotgun, taking a mid-body bead on Bill. Julia is frantic and screams beside herself with fear,

'No! No! You cannot do this. You know he's innocent and it must have been this beast of a son here who was responsible for attacking me. '

Her eyes are wide and her hair dishevelled giving her the appearance of a wild woman. Mr Johnson hesitates at this apparition not knowing what she might do next, but just then they hear the sound of police klaxons that distract them all. Bill is the first to collect his wits and grabbing the pitchfork that is near him, he hurls it at the farmer piercing him in the thigh. Mr Johnson utters a howl of pain and drops the shotgun which lands on the floor and sets off the second barrel. The full collective force of the cartridge hits Frank squarely in the face destroying his head completely. Police rush into the barn to a horrific sight which they don't know how to interpret. There is a headless, dead man, another seriously injured with a pitchfork sticking out from his leg and the prisoner, whom they are hunting. Bill is grabbed and handcuffed immediately and then Inspector Walsh spots Julia who can't move or speak at what she has just seen. He throws his coat over her shoulders and gently leads her into the farm kitchen. There she tells him the whole story and concludes by saying that it must have been Frank all along who was her mysterious attacker. The detective is fully aware of the details of the first investigation and says there is only one problem with this explanation and it lies with the discovery of Bill's pocketknife after she'd been raped. But then Julia remembers that Bill was looking for his pocketknife before he left the farmhouse with her that night but neither of them could find it. It was usually in his coat pocket that had been hanging up in the hallway. Bill had neglected to provide this information during the shock of the initial enquiry and trial. He simply thought it must have dropped out of his pocket earlier in the evening whilst he was walking up to the farmhouse. It becomes clear to the Inspector that Frank must have stolen it and thrown it by the side of the unconscious Julia to incriminate Bill.

The following week, Inspector Walsh returns to the evidence and the trial transcript and is convinced of Bill's innocence. The Governor is glad to contribute his own positive view of Bill's character and when they present their conclusions to a local High Court judge, Bill is released. During the same week, Mr Johnson suffers a fatal heart attack never having fully recovered from the shock of his own part in Frank's death. Julia inherits the farm as the only remaining close relative and legal charge of the Johnsons.

Julia and Bill are married within the month and take up residence in the little farm below the beacon on the Wrekin.

The End.

Historical note: After a number of aircraft crashes into the Wrekin, a beacon emitting an intermittent red light was erected on its northern summit in 1940. This was removed in 1960. However, after a local survey in favour of its restoration, a new beacon was erected to commemorate the millennium in 2000.

The Isolate

I have never seen him. I know he's there. I have felt the sinister menacing strength of his presence. I shiver at the possibility of meeting him. His power resonates from the signs he has put up,

Enter On Pain of Death - You Will Die

These chilling messages are daubed on old pieces of wood or faded black tarpaulin on the tumbledown walls of the old cottage, but they are especially potent on the black ramshackle shed where the white paint stands out larger-than-life.

Then, there are the dogs. Three huge black slavering Doberman. The first time I encountered them my adrenaline system went into overdrive. The hairs on my head and neck tingled and went rigid. My spine was a conduit that yelled DANGER! to my extremities and I felt the blood drain from them as my body prepared itself for fight or flight. Deep within my childhood memories was an episode that gave me strength. A neighbour kept a vicious Alsatian and whenever I passed the drive it always attacked me, an adolescent male teenager, someone who must show submission before being allowed to pass. I spent weeks mentally wrestling with this nightmare until I summoned up the courage to confront the brute head on, lashing out with my feet and fists. It never bothered me again. Remembering this, I stood stock still and turned towards these devils and as one crashed against the rickety old wooden fence I noticed with considerable relief they were chained to a ring on the wall. One day, however, for whatever reason I never knew, the chains were lengthened and there they stood before me in the middle of the road, waiting, three hounds of hell ready to tear me limb from limb. Again, I stood my ground and with hot and cold shivers flooding my body, but not a sign of fear on the outside, walked straight through a wall of continuous barking.

I wondered at the legality of those ominous signs. I couldn't be the only one to have seen them. There were two other houses within the vicinity, both of which had guard dogs but presented nothing like the terror of the isolated house on the south-west corner of the Wrekin. Had anyone reported this to the police? Had anyone ever been attacked by the dogs? Why was this tolerated? I ask around one or two people I know in the area but they seem to know nothing.

From time to time, passing to and fro on the small road on the west side of the Wrekin, I have seen a slender figure wearing an old fashioned khaki gabardine Macintosh. He wears a woollen bonnet with sidepieces so his face isn't readily visible. He clutches an old umbrella that he never seems to use even when the rain is torrential. Is this him? Where is he going? Is he simply off to the shops? If I stopped him and offered a lift, would he accept or politely decline in a refined, educated voice? Or, would he grunt and say something unintelligible?

He keeps me awake at nights. Why do I care about him? Perhaps he's a raving psychopath and I should just pass by on the other side lest he do me some dreadful harm. Would he welcome the attentions of another or see it as a gross intrusion, which his messages suggest? Perhaps he really craves company and is the only child of elderly dysfunctional parents who passed away long ago and he doesn't know how to make contact with the outside world successfully? It may be that he is an old soldier damaged beyond repair in some long forgotten overseas conflict, whose name appears somewhere on a list of volunteers or recruits.

Sometimes I dream of him sitting there all alone in the midst of a bare room on a single chair with a double-barrelled shotgun, which he aims full square into my face before he dissolves and I wake up in a cold sweat. Or at others, I see a room scattered with papers and piled high with books, and in the midst of all this a tiny wizened, bespectacled and deeply preoccupied old man scrawling frantically away on an ancient yellow parchment that is covered in unknown symbols and strange diagrams, holding the answers to life's mysteries. If I could just see more clearly, I might learn the answer to immortality, time travel or how to visit the distant stars in an instant.

The world has rotated a few more dozen times round the sun since then. All is gone but the shell of the building that was home to my enigma. No messages, no dogs. Presently, unseen hands have been at work until the old cottage has become a sizeable new house with a large rectangular west facing window. I look in. It is sterile and lifeless. I feel no presence, benign nor malevolent. One day a drive appears, the old worm eaten fence has gone but there is still no one there. I don't linger any more. I don't await the terrifying onrush of the black dogs. Can it be that I miss this one sided struggle with my nemesis and now it is gone, all is flat? I move on saddened by the world's uniformity. The magic is no more.

The End.

Folklore: a personal experience.

Bibliography

M J Angold, G C Baugh, Marjorie M Chibnall, D C Cox, D T W Price, Margaret Tomlinson and B S Trinder, 'House of Cistercian monks: Abbey of Buildwas', in *A History of the County of Shropshire: Volume 2*, ed. A T Gaydon and R B Pugh (London, 1973), pp. 50-59. *British History Online* http://www.british-history.ac.uk/vch/salop/vol2/pp50-59 [accessed 22 November 2018].

Doomsday Book (2017) Domesday Book Online 1999 to 2017 <accessed on 15 November 2018>

Historic England (2004) Large multivallate and univallate hillforts, a round barrow, a Late Bronze Age settlement and WWII military remains, on The Wrekin.

Shropshire History (2015) Roman Shropshire <Shropshire history.com, accessed 15 November 2018>

Time Team (2013) Time Team Kynnersley Arms, Ironbridge Gorge S09 E05 [YouTube video]

About the Author

Retired college lecturer, Noel Conway has lived and worked in and around the Wrekin, Shropshire, for the past 38 years. He is acquainted with its public and secret ways. In 2014 he was diagnosed with motor neurone disease and given only a short time to live. However, he has outlived this prediction but is now dependent totally on carers day and night not being able to move his arms or legs. He relives what was a very active and physical life which included walking the highways and byways of his beloved Shropshire, cycling, rock climbing and mountaineering in the UK and the Alps, as well as being a keen skier. Since 2016 he has been an ardent campaigner to legalise assisted dying in the UK becoming the chief legal claimant until his case was rejected by the Supreme Court. Since retiring in

2014 he has devoted himself increasingly to writing and has self published a book of poetry entitled *A Life in Words*, available on Amazon Books. He is now just completing his memoirs that include his recent legal fight as well as his struggle with MND, which will be coming out in the New Year and called *Hard Day's Journey into Night.*

15586149R00072

Printed in Great Britain
by Amazon